The MIGHTY FROG

Guy Bass

stripes

Who's Who in Kingdomland

FROG
Alien Prince,
self-proclaimed saviour
of the world, rebel
without a pause, wielder
of the invincible magic
sword Basil Rathbone.

BUTTERCUP
Frog's best friend who
raised him from an egg
and kept him safe at The
Edge of the End of the
World, keeper of secrets.

SHERIFF
EXPLOSION
Frog's trusty yet
reluctant steed.

THE RAREWOLF
Ancient beast, guardian of the
world and god of the storms,
last of his kind, bit of a grump.

KRYL
Kroakan traitor, Frog's Keeper,
pilot of the farship that brought
Frog from the planet Kroakas
to Kingdomland.

PRINCESS RAINBOW

Heir to the throne of Kingdomland, daughter of the King and Queen of Everything, wearer of sparkly dresses.

MAN-LOR

Furry-panted, barbarian protector of Princess Rainbow, secret writer of poetry.

Gone But Not Forgotten:

THE QUEEN OF EVERYTHING

Magisterial Monarch of Kingdomland.

THE KING OF EVERYTHING

Kingdomland's kindly King.

THE WIZARD OLDASDUST

Kingdomland's royal wizard, adviser to Princess Rainbow, caster of spells, wearer of impractically tall hats.

The Bragons

NIGEL THE BRAGON
Bafflingly boastful Enemy
of Kingdomland.

OLD 'N' GRAHAM
The oldest and most
bearded of the bragons.

SUSAN
Bluest and most
tea-fixated bragon.

The Kroakan Army

KING KROAK
Ruler of Kroakas and the Army
of a Thousand Sons, merciless
intergalactic conqueror,
Frog's dad.

MAJOR KRUNG
King Kroak's
calm and collected
right-hand Kroakan.

GENERAL KURG
Captured commander of the
513th Kroakan invasion fleet,
failed space invader.

KROOP & KRUD
Senseless sentries.

Once Upon
the End of the World...

The Astownding, Astonishing, Legendary Legend of Prince Fro

What Happuns After the Stuff that Happuned Before This

One upon a tyme there was a prince callec FROG. Frog grew up on a farty little island with his best frend BUTTERCUP just eating burpy vegetabuls and not doing much.

Buttercup toled Frog that he was supposed to be the prince of a magicul wurld called Kingdomland, which wasunt really true. That job was alreddy taken by a prinsess called Rainbow who was HORRIBUL at first but now is OK, I suppose.

Buttercup also toled Frog that the wurld had ended, which wasunt really true either, and she didunt menshun that Frog was ackshully the prince of an outer space ~~plant~~ planet called KROAKAS, which was filled up with alien KROAKANS and rooled by an evil space villun called KING KROAK.

King Kroak sent his evil space invaiders to a ~~thowsand thowzund thouzand~~ whole bunch of wurlds so they could conker them. Frog was supposed to conker Kingdomland but he said No Way! I will save the wurld instead in the mighty champion style. So he defeeted the Kroakans in no time flat. But then they came back. And this time there were LODES of them.

They blew everything to pieces and made trubble all over Kingdomland. So Frog made a vow that he would defeet all the invaiders even if it took a whole week.

Soon roomers started spredding among the Kroakan invaiders abowt a MISTERIOUS Kroakan rebbul who appeared from the darkness when the invaiders least expected it and defeeted them with his might. The rebbul started saving the world one bit at a time. His lejend spred like butter on a hot turnip.

He was so mighty no one could stop him.

He was so mighty he could not even stop himself!

And he was getting mighterier by the minute.

The Swamp of Notable Odour

"Who's there?"

The Kroakan sentry drew his sunder-gun. He peered nervously into the darkness of the swamp. "Show yourself, in the name of King Kroak!"

"It's me, you *slurm*," came a cry. "Put that away before you hurt someone."

"Kroop?" whimpered the sentry.

From behind a gnarled tree emerged another Kroakan. The other-worldly pair looked almost identical, with green skin, wide hairless heads and bulbous amphibian eyes. They even wore the same sleek oil-black armour, which glinted in the light of the three moons.

"Of course it's Kroop! Who did you expect — King Kroak?" said the second Kroakan. "Your shift is up, Krud."

"You're my relief? What a relief! I almost relieved myself," said Krud. He pointed to the ten saucer-shaped spaceships parked behind them in a clearing in the forest. "Security of the traceship fleet is all yours, Kroop ... and not a mikron too soon. I hate sentry duty — and not just this stinking swamp. Something about this planet gives me the *gwirms*."

"You worry too much, Krud," said Kroop. "We'll have this mudball conquered in no time. The natives are always trouble at first, but they come round soon enough. And if they don't, we blast them to atoms. The system works!"

"It's not the natives I'm worried about," said Krud, with a shiver. "It's *him*."

"'Him'? Oh, Kroak's Elbow, not this again," sighed Kroop. "I'm not listening to any more of your guff, Krud. This 'rebel' of yours is a *myth*."

"But what if the legends are true? What if he's the lost Kroakan prince, fighting against his own army, picking off our squadrons one by one?" whimpered Krud, his eyes darting frantically about. "They say he appears at night, riding on a thundercloud… They say he's taller than a thorg, with arms as thick as a zerk's tentaclaws, eyes redder than a grorn's left buttock and legs longer than a flooble's—"

"Nonsense! Your brain's in a stink," tutted Kroop.

"And fire breath and mind control and acid for blood!" added Krud.

"Would you shut your communication

hole?" Kroop snapped. "For the last time, there is no—"

CRACK!

The snapping of burnt twigs was enough to make both sentries draw their sunder-guns.

"It's him! It's the rebel!" cried Krud. "He's come to show us the folly of war by killing us!"

CRACK!

CRACK!

"Shh! It's ... it's coming closer!" hissed Kroop, aiming at the trees. "Set guns to sunder! Prepare to—"

"Baa."

A grubby mess of wool and legs emerged from the treeline. Krud and Kroop breathed a mutual sigh of relief.

"What is it? Looks like a puff of smoke," noted Krud, peering at the curious creature.

"Baa," the sheep bleated, staring blankly.

"Whatever it is, it doesn't seem to be doing any harm. Let's blast it to atoms," Kroop replied. They aimed their sunder-guns at the sheep. "OK, on three. One … two … thr—"

BOOM!

The sentries spun around, their ear hollows ringing from the sound. The traceships were ablaze. They exploded one after the other, collapsing like dominos, metal screeching against metal, torrents of flame belching into the air. In seconds, all the sentries could see was fire.

"Green alert! We're under attack!" screamed Kroop. "Open fire! Destroy everything that's not already destroyed!"

As if on cue, sunder-beams streaked out from the inferno, blasting the sentries' weapons from their hands. A moment later, a figure emerged from the heart of the blaze. He was clad in a long fur cape, which burned and smouldered. In one hand he wielded a sunder-gun, and in the other a gleaming sword. And his skin...

...His skin was green.

"The rebel prince! He's come for us!" squeaked Krud. "And he's shorter than I expected!"

Kroop and Krud watched in horror as the figure strode towards them, flames licking at his ankles. He brushed ash from his Kroakan armour, its black surface painted white.

"You … you don't scare us!" cried Kroop. "We are Kroakans! We are fearless! We—"

"We surrender!" Krud pleaded. "Please don't kill us!"

"I'm not going to kill you. I'm going to defeat the bumbles out of you," came the reply. "And then I'm going to defeat the bumbles out of your whole invasion."

"What are you?" whispered Kroop.

The rebel glared at him, reflected flames flickering in his eyes.

"I am *Frog*," he growled. Then he thought

for a moment. "Or Frog the Mighty, or The Amazing Frog, or The Frog of Steel, or Frog the *Defeatinator*! Yoiks, I dunno ... which one sounds best?"

"Baa..." sighed the sheep.

The Defeat All Foes Team

The sun was beginning to rise over Kingdomland. The sky churned with black smoke as far as the eye could see, but dawn light still broke through to the swamp.

"Whiffs and stinks! I'm s'posed to smell like strawbleflowers, not pong gobbins," grumbled Princess Rainbow. The heir to the throne of Kingdomland was a plump five-year-old in a rose pink dress decorated with tiny diamonds. She was perched on the shoulders of her bodyguard, Man-Lor, a mammoth of a man clad in little more than a furry loincloth, and toting the bound Krud and Kroop under each arm.

"Swamp smells like Man-Lor's toilet," noted Man-Lor. "And Man-Lor's toilet does not flush."

"Baa," agreed Frog's trusty steed, Sheriff Explosion the sheep, as he perched on a tree branch to avoid the stagnant swamp water.

"Take that!" Frog cried, hacking madly at the decimated Kroakan traceships with his sword. "Taste the SWISH! and Ka-SLICE! of Basil Rathbone, the most unbreakable sword in the world! Eat the justice! Eat it!"

"Silly Greeny," huffed the princess. "Why is he smash-ting everything that's already been smash-ted?"

"Baa," offered Sheriff Explosion.

"Because Frog is the son of King Kroak," came the more helpful reply. From behind a tree emerged Kryl, a slender Kroakan decked in flowing robes, with long antennae protruding from her forehead. "The King intended all of his one thousand sons to be merciless conquerors."

"So does that mean Greeny's going bad?" asked Princess Rainbow, peering suspiciously at Frog's white-daubed Kroakan armour. "He's even starting to *dress* bad."

"No, of course not. I'm Frog's Keeper, Princess. I know him. He's…" Kryl trailed off, watching Frog attack the traceships.

"Mightiness pie in your face!" roared Frog.

"Well, he *is* smash-ting the ay'lun invaders at least," declared the princess. She put her hands on her hips. "With the help of the Pretty Princess Lovely Biscuit Team."

"That is not our name!" cried Frog, hopping down from the traceship wreckage into the waist-deep water. "I already *gave* us a name that inspires lip-trembles and pant-wetting! We are … the Defeat All Foes Team!"

"That's daft," replied the princess. "It ackshully spells it. D-A-F-T."

"That's not important!" snapped Frog. He swished his sword in the air. "What's important is that Basil Rathbone here is spoiling for another fight and *I'm* spoiling to spoil the Kroakans. I'll spoil them to pieces!"

"Perhaps we should get these prisoners back to the royal palace before the rest of their squadron turns up..." suggested Kryl.

"Baa," agreed Sheriff Explosion.

"Why do we always have to take them to *my* house?" groaned Princess Rainbow. "What if they *ex-scape* and steal my dresses?"

"We've got to put them somewhere, Princess *Brain-Slow*," tutted Frog. "Anyway, we've stolen enough Kroakan prison domes to hold a million Kroakans ... maybe even a hundred."

"As long as no one finds them," added Kryl. "The more prisoners we have, the harder they are to conceal."

"Which is why the King and Queen are keeping an eye on them," sighed Frog, suddenly impatient. "Look, I've been doing world-saving all week and I've captured bumbles knows how many Kroakans. I'm getting *mighterier* by the minute! Even my kroak cloak is more skilled up. I can turn myself one hundred per cent invisible now — even my undies!"

"Yes, but—" Kryl began.

"You said we should run and hide from the invaders," added Frog sternly. "You didn't believe I could do it, and I did it!"

"*We* did it," added Princess Rainbow. "Pretty Princess Lovely Biscuit—"

"That is *not* our name!" snapped Frog.

CHAPTER TWENTY-SIX

The Ambush

The Defeet All Foes Teem Song

When invaiders invaide from owter space
We are here to punch their face
We don't wait for an invitaishun
We hand out defeet like a generuss donaishun

D-A-F-T!
Defeat All Foes Team!
Smash the badness
And eat lots of proteen

So skilled up it makes your hed spin
We're docturs with a cleer prescripshun
Admit defeet cos we're the winner
Eat our justice like it's dinner

D-A-F-T!
Defeet All Foes Teem!
Smash the badness
And eat taisty ice creem

Frog is leeder, with Sheriff Explosion!
Basil Rathbone is causing a commoshun
And some others too have come along
To save the day and sing this song
Yeah, yeah, yeah, yeah (fade out)

"'And some others too'?" complained Princess Rainbow. "Your stupid song only sings about you and your stuff!"

"Pfff – I don't see you making up a full-on team song," tutted Frog loudly.

He and the Defeat All Foes Team had been walking all afternoon – out of the Swamp of Notable Odour, over the Fountain Mountains and through Dillydally Valley towards the palace.

"That's because team songs are silly and stupid and— *My house!*" the princess cried. As they crossed the ridge, the royal palace of Kingdomland came into view. Despite being devastated by the Kroakan invaders, the white-stone citadel remained an imposing sight. It seemed to glow in the mid-morning light.

"I'm going to cuddle my mummy and daddy until they 'splode!" declared Princess Rainbow, as they hurried across the bridge to the makeshift palace gates.

"Cuddles shmuddles! This is champion business," Frog exclaimed, overtaking the princess and pushing open the gates. He strode inside what remained of a once-great hall. "Three cheers for the Defeat All Foes Team, back from defeating badness! Polished sandwiches and foot rubs all round!"

"Where should Man-Lor take space

gobbins?" asked Man-Lor, Kroop and Krud still held firmly under his massive arms.

"To the throne room!" Frog said. "We'll deliver them straight to the King and Queen — I can't wait to see the looks on their faces…"

Everyone followed as Frog marched through the hall and into the throne room. Long curtains draped the walls and in the middle of the room, at the top of a grand flight of stairs, were three thrones. Atop their seats sat the Queen of Everything, looking as regal as ever in her golden finery, and her husband the King of Everything, a portly old codger with food in his beard.

"Daddy! Mummy!" squealed Princess Rainbow. She rushed up the steps and hugged them tightly.

"So what have you been doing while we've

been out catching Kroakans and saving up the world?" scoffed Frog, striking a pose at the foot of the stairs. "Shining up the royal crowns and twiddling your— Wuuh?"

Frog looked down. On the floor was a large pile of grey-black dust. There was another a little further away, and another ... a dozen at least, dotted all over the throne room.

"Get the princess out of here, Frog – *now*," whispered Kryl, drawing her bow from behind her back.

Frog glanced up to see Princess Rainbow hugging her parents.

"Mummy? Daddy? Why aren't you hugging back?" said the princess. She looked up at their faces and gasped. Their eyes were pupil-less, and as black as coal.

"Hail, Kroak," said the King and Queen in unison.

Before Frog knew what was happening, a
dozen Kroakans had emerged from behind
the curtains. He drew his sword.

"Baa?" bleated Sheriff Explosion.

"It's an ambush!" cried Kryl. "The
prisoners are free!"

"Yoiks!" cried Frog, swinging his sword wildly. "Get behind me! Get—"

Frog felt a blow on the back of the head. His brain rattled in his skull and he saw the floor of the throne room rush up to meet him. He landed with a *thud* and heard his sword clang to the ground next to him. With his head spinning, Frog tried to trigger his kroak cloak to turn himself invisible when he felt himself hoisted into the air by both arms.

"By the Clenched Fist, hold him!" roared a voice. Frog looked up to see a huge armoured figure step forward. He was the biggest Kroakan in the room, and Frog recognized him immediately.

"General Kurg!" Frog cried. He gave his former general a stern glare.

"Surprised to see me?" growled the general.

"I suppose you would be, since you blasted my squadron with thunder and lightning, destroyed my *bipods*, locked me in a stinking cage and left me in this palace to rot!"

"It was better than you deserved for all your badness!" growled Frog. "Now, let us go or I'll defeat you to pieces!"

"I'm sorry. Did I not make it clear that I don't take orders from you any more, O Prince?" sneered the general. "I've been given a second chance – and I'm not going to slurm it up. Now surrender!"

"Surrender? Bumdrops to that!" roared Frog. "I'll punch your face!"

"Look around, Frog … your little rebellion is over," said General Kurg, gesturing across the room. To his left, Frog saw Kryl, Man-Lor and Sheriff Explosion, surrounded by Kroakan troopers. To his right, the black-eyed

King and Queen dragged the princess roughly down the steps of the throne. Then the Queen picked up Frog's sword and held the blade to Princess Rainbow's neck.

"Queen, have you all gone loopy-doopy? That's the princess! *Your* princess!" Frog cried. "And that's *my* invincible sword – give it back!"

"Hail, Kroak," replied the Queen, her black eyes expressionless and cold.

"What the bumbles?" blurted Frog. He glowered at General Kurg. "What did you do to them?"

"Just a little *brain-slaving*, O Prince," explained the general, holding up what looked like a small black pebble. "One of these slave-nodes delivers a concentrated injection of pure loyalty. Instant slave."

"Mummy? Daddy?" said Princess Rainbow,

peering nervously up at the Queen. "Did they slave your brains?"

"Hail, Kroak," replied her parents in unison.

"And since you were *stupid* enough to leave our equipment lying around the palace, we had sufficient nodes to set up this nifty little ambush," continued General Kurg, drawing a sunder-gun. "And enough weapons to reduce the rest of the natives to *dust*."

Frog glanced down at the dust piles on the floor. "Y-you slayed the royal army … Captain Camperlash … all of them!"

"Every last insignificant life form!" replied the general. "And if you and your friends want to avoid a similar fate, you'll do exactly as you're told."

"Argh! I'll defeat the boots off you!

I'll defeat you into soup!" roared Frog. "I'll defeat you and undefeat you so I can defeat you again! I'll—"

"Moons of Moonos! I forgot how much you talk, Frog," grunted General Kurg. He dragged the sentries, Krud and Kroop, from under Man-Lor's arms and dangled them in the air. "You two! Arm up and bring the prisoners — we meet at the rendezvous point in twenty krons! Let's move out, by Kroakas!"

The Ocean in the Sky

"I command we stop being priz'ners this instant!" huffed Princess Rainbow, as Kroop and Krud marched the Defeat All Foes Team through the Desert of Sandy Toes.

"We're giving the orders!" yelled Krud. "Shut your communication hole!"

A few steps ahead, Frog and Kryl followed General Kurg as he led the way to the rendezvous point.

"I don't understand," whispered Frog. "How the bumbles did General Kurg escape?"

"I'm not sure," replied Kryl. "He couldn't have done it without help – and someone's given him new orders. But who?"

"General!" cried Kroop suddenly, pointing to the sky.

Frog looked up to see a dark shape descend from the heavens – a Kroakan traceship. The ship's retro-rockets sent a storm of sand swirling around them as the craft landed with a crunch on the ground. The door opened and a tongue-like stairwell snaked out from inside.

"All aboard!" boomed General Kurg. "Death to all dawdlers."

"*Fine* . . . but I have to be back for teatime," added Princess Rainbow. "We're having plumberry pie."

Frog and the other prisoners were led up the steps, then herded to the back of the traceship.

"By the Buttocks of Time, what are you waiting for?" said General Kurg, prodding the pilot. "We don't want to keep King Kroak waiting."

"King Kroak?" repeated Kryl, as the traceship jetted into the sky. "Impossible! This ship will never make it all the way to Kroakas. We'd need a farship with enough stasis pods to—"

"Kroakas? Who said anything about going to Kroakas?" laughed General Kurg. "The King is not as far away as you think."

Frog saw the colour drain from Kryl's face.

"General, please don't do this!" she pleaded. "If you hand Frog over to King Kroak, you'll be sentencing him to death!"

"By the Boot of Oppression, death will be the least of his worries when King Kroak gets his hands on him," replied the general.

"Pfff — don't worry, Kryl, I'll defeat the cheese out of General Kurg any second now," said a defiant Frog, although nothing sprung to mind. He didn't even have his invincible sword or sunder-gun, never mind an excellent and *bold-venturous* plan. He peered out of the pilot's view-screens as the traceship climbed higher, beyond the layer of black smoke, soaring upwards until it was clear of the clouds. Then, in the far distance, Frog spotted something glistening. He peered closer.

It was a waterfall, tumbling down through the sky.

"What the ... what?" he muttered. "I know that waterfall..."

"Baa?" bleated Sheriff Explosion.

"I *fell down* that waterfall! That's how I ended up in Kingdomland," Frog continued in a whisper. "But that means..."

"General!" cried the traceship pilot. "There's something up ahead. It's not registering on my scanners, but ... it's everywhere!"

Above them, floating in mid-air, was a vast ocean of water. It stretched for miles in every direction, glinting silver in the sunlight.

"No *way*," muttered Frog. "Is that... Is that the Inbetween?"

"By the Plunder, go through it! We have a schedule to keep," growled General Kurg. The traceship ploughed into the water with a jarring thud. In less than a moment, they were submerged.

"Silly water… You can't have sea in the sky," noted Princess Rainbow, watching a school of whistle fish swim past the view-screen. "It must have gotted lost."

"I can see the surface, General," assured the pilot. "We should be clear in a few seconds."

Frog tapped his fingertips together.

"Wait a miniscule, I think I just— Yep! I just thought of a plan … and it might be my most excellent and bold-venturous plan yet," he whispered. "Come on, everybody – we're *leaving*."

"Baa?" bleated Sheriff Explosion.

"Clamp it, you deviants!" hissed Kroop, pointing his sunder-gun. "I thought I told you to shut your communication holes!"

"And I told *you* I was going to defeat the bumbles out of you," replied Frog. He activated his kroak cloak, disappearing in front of Kroop and Krud's eyes.

"He's cloaked!" cried Kroop. "Shoot him!"

"How can I, if I can't see him?" howled Krud. "*You* shoot him!"

"I'm not shooting if you're not shooting!" yelled Kroop. "We'll shoot together! One ... two..."

"Three!" shouted the invisible Frog. He ducked as both sentries fired at what they thought was Frog ... and blasted each other across the room.

"Who's firing? We're in a pressurized container, by Kroakas!" barked General Kurg from the cockpit.

Frog reappeared. He scooped up Sheriff Explosion and grabbed one of the sentry's fallen sunder-guns. He turned to Kryl and grinned. Then he took aim at the cockpit window.

"Oh *no*," Kryl whispered, grabbing Princess Rainbow. "Take a deep breath, Princess!"

"Who wants to go for a swim?" grinned Frog – and pulled the trigger.

BOOM!

The Return to the Island

A bolt of energy shot out from Frog's sunder-gun, shattering the cockpit window. There was a deafening *FWHUUSH!* as a torrent of water rushed into the traceship. General Kurg and the pilot took the brunt of the force and were slammed against the back wall. Frog hung on to his sheep as the churning water battered and buffeted him. In seconds, the traceship was totally flooded.

Frog steadied himself, remembering how to breathe underwater. He spotted Kryl, swimming towards the shattered cockpit as she clung to Princess Rainbow. Frog pushed off against a wall – grabbing Man-Lor by the loincloth as the barbarian floated helplessly by – and rushed through the hole.

Frog looked up and saw sunlight glinting on the surface of the water. With another few kicks, he propelled himself and his passengers to the surface, bursting out of the water with a *POOSHH*!

"Baa!" bleated Sheriff Explosion in terror.

Frog held his sheep tightly as Man-Lor spat out mouthfuls of water.

"Hold still, Sheriff! I've got you!" cried Frog, the waves lapping against his face. A moment later, Kryl burst out of the water with a gasping Princess Rainbow.

"*That* was your excellent plan?" cried Kryl. "We could have been killed!"

"Bad Greeny!" gasped Princess Rainbow.

"Wasn't it *awe-mazing*?" laughed Frog, an excited school of whistle fish dancing out of the water around him. "Sometimes I'm so mighty ... it's..."

Frog trailed off. He'd seen something in the distance – a small island in the water.

"That island ... that's my island," he muttered. "I knew it! This *is* the Inbetween!"

"What's the *in-bee-teen*?" coughed Princess Rainbow.

"It's home! My home!" replied Frog. "This is an even more excellent plan than I planned … everyone follow me!"

"Baa!" bleated Sheriff Explosion, as Frog began to swim, holding the panicking sheep above the water.

Man-Lor and Kryl followed behind, with Princess Rainbow clinging to Kryl's neck. Finally, they reached the shore and struggled on to dry land.

"Baa!" bleated Sheriff Explosion again, springing on to the soil with relief.

Frog stared up at the house. It was exactly as he'd left it only a month ago. The Kroakans had ignored the island – that meant Buttercup was safe! He could almost smell the burpy turnips boiling away… Almost hear his best friend singing tuneless lullabies as she stirred the cooking pot.

"Buttercup!" Frog cried. "It's me! It's Frog!"

"Frog, wait," began Kryl. "I have to tell you some—"

"Baa!"

At the terrified bleat of his trusty steed, Frog spun around. General Kurg's traceship had emerged from the Inbetween, water cascading from its hull. It hovered ominously in the air a few paces from the shore. Through the blasted cockpit Frog saw General Kurg at the controls.

"You just can't keep a good traceship down!" the general roared, as the ship's sunder-cannons glowed with green energy.

"Everybody, move!" cried Frog. "He's going to—"

The sunder-beams' shrieks filled the air. Frog prepared for the worst – but the beams passed straight over his head ... blowing the house into a thousand pieces.

The Truth About Buttercup

"UUuuuhHRRRF!" cried Frog, blown off his feet by the force of the explosion. He skidded to a halt on the shore and lay there for a moment, his ears ringing.

"Buh... Buttercup?" Frog murmured, looking up at the house. It was gone — reduced to flaming rubble. He struggled to his feet and began stumbling towards it. "BUTTERCUP!"

Frog clambered over the burning wreckage, blinded by smoke and ash. He heaved chunks of wood and brick, desperately calling Buttercup's name. Princess Rainbow and Man-Lor joined in, scouring the ruins. Even Sheriff Explosion tried to help, clopping awkwardly over the rubble and bleating loudly.

"Consider *that* your final warning, O Prince," said a voice.

Frog turned to see the traceship land roughly on the shore. The door slid open and General Kurg strode down the steps. "Now, get back on the traceship. King Kroak is waiting for you."

"*You*... You killed her! You killed Buttercup!" Frog screamed in rage, his eyes flooding red.

General Kurg drew his sunder-gun but Frog was too fast — he drew his own gun and fired, blasting the general's weapon from his hands. Frog's finger hovered over the trigger again ... but this time he aimed at the general's head.

"Frog, wait!" cried Kryl. "Don't do it!"

"Listen to your Keeper, O Prince!" cried General Kurg. "Let's not do anything rash..."

"He killed my best friend!" Frog howled, tears welling in his eyes. "And I'm going to kill him back!"

54

"But he didn't kill her!" cried Kryl, as Frog began to squeeze the trigger. "Look!"

Frog's eyes flashed towards Kryl. He saw her vanish — to be replaced by a shimmering haze. A moment later someone else entirely emerged. A *human* someone, with kindly brown eyes and a rosy-lipped smile spreading across a plump, pink face. Frog's mouth fell open.

"*Buttercup…?*" he blurted. "How did… Where did you… What the *bumbles*?"

"Magic!" cried Princess Rainbow excitedly.

"Not quite … kroak cloak," said Buttercup. She turned to Frog. "I'm Kroakan, just like you, Frog. I should have told you, but…"

"You're Kryl? I mean, you're Buttercup? I mean, you're *ButterKryl*?" Frog rambled, lowering his sunder-gun.

"It's a long story, Frog, and it began before we ever came to this island," explained Buttercup. The air shimmered again, and in an instant Buttercup became Kryl once more. "Back when the farship crashed in the lake of the royal palace, back when you were still an egg. I told you that you had floated out of the ship … that I had lost you. But in fact I saw Princess Rainbow pluck the egg out of the water and take it back to the palace."

"It's not my fault you looked like treasure," tutted the princess.

"I had to get you back," continued Kryl. "I used the farship's lexicron to absorb the native language, the kroak cloak to disguise myself as a human, and the UnSlumber to infiltrate the King and Queen's dreams and persuade them that they needed a new loyal subject. Once inside, I waited for an opportunity to steal back the egg, but it didn't come until the rarewolf attacked the castle."

"The rarewolf?" uttered Frog. "He thought I was going to make the world end, so he wanted to eat me."

"In the commotion, I stole back the egg and fled," continued Kryl. "But a few hours later, the rarewolf tracked down my scent. He would have swallowed you there and then, but I begged him not to. He agreed to spare your life on one condition: that you never set foot in Kingdomland. He used his power over the winds to carry us to the Inbetween, to the island in the sky ... and left us there."

"I don't get it," Frog said. "If you couldn't tell me I was a *Kroakan* prince, why did you tell me I was a prince at all?"

"I had to tell you something! I had denied you your destiny," Kryl sighed. "You were born to rule. You are a son of— Look out!"

Frog spun around. He saw General Kurg leaping towards him, his massive fist swinging towards his head...

...And then the world turned to black.

The Return to the UnSlumber

"WUuUH?"

Frog opened his eyes. He sat up and looked around. He was lying on a long, raised bed in a round room, lit green like the inside of a traceship. "Where the bumbles am I?"

Frog hopped off the bed and spotted a circular black door at the far end of the chamber. He made his way towards it, and the door opened like a blossoming flower. Frog wandered through.

"Yoiks!"

He was standing at the top of a great tower, higher than any mountain he'd ever seen. Far below him Frog saw row after row of armoured Kroakan troopers — an army, poised and ready for battle. Behind them stood hundreds of bipods, the Kroakan's towering, tentacled machines of war. And in the air above them hovered a fleet of deadly traceships.

"Hail, Frog!" the army chanted in unison.

"Hail … me?" Frog whispered.

"So it would seem," said a voice.

Frog turned, and his jaw fell open. Behind him in the open doorway, he saw a cloaked figure, shrouded in shadow. Atop the figure's head, Frog noticed the silhouette of a spiked crown.

"K-king Kroak?" he muttered, his blood running cold.

"At your service! Not literally – I mean, I *am* the ruler of the universe," replied King Kroak. "I just thought I'd drop in and say 'Hi'."

"Drop in?" said Frog. He slapped his forehead with his hand. "Oh bumdrops, this is the UnSlumber, isn't it? I'm asleep and you're mentally sticking your nose into my dream business… Ugh! UnSlumbering's just a way to give people bad news without actually having to face their face."

"You may have a point there," laughed King Kroak. "But once you can enter the dreams of others, you can do all sorts of clever stuff. Like convincing those weak-minded natives to free General Kurg and the troopers you imprisoned…"

"You did that?" blurted Frog, as King Kroak stepped out of the gloom. "No fair!

It took me days to catch all those—"

Frog gasped. Not only was King Kroak suddenly much smaller, but he was also Frog's exact double. It was like looking in a mirror.

"Yoiks!" cried Frog.

The King inspected his hands. "How about that?" he said. "In your dreams, I, the supreme ruler of the entire universe, look exactly like *you*. Talk about big-headed…"

"Look, can we do this later? I really need to wake up," huffed Frog. "I've got a whole world to save thanks to you."

"Save? You *really* got your brain stunk," the King laughed. "I'm going to be honest with you, Frog. After all the trouble you've caused I would have been happy to see you disintegrated. I mean, fighting against the Kroakan army! That is not the sort of behaviour I expect from a son of mine. But then I decided to poke around your dreams. I've been visiting you in the UnSlumber for days now."

"What? Stay *out* of my sleeps, you weirdo!" Frog growled.

"Did you know you've been having this same dream for five nights running? This great army you see before you ... this is the dream of a *conqueror*," said King Kroak. "We're more alike than you realize, Frog. I've decided there's hope for you yet. I'm giving you a second chance."

"Wait, I don't want all this — it's just a stupid dream!" snapped Frog. "I'm nothing like you! I'm anti-conquering and anti-slaying."

"Pfff — I just tripped over a memory of you trying to *execute* General Kurg," replied King Kroak. "Doesn't seem very anti-slaying to me."

"That's ... that's different," Frog said.

"No, *you're* different ... different from my other nine hundred and ninety-nine sons," said King Kroak, taking another step towards him. "Look, Frog, I'll explain everything in good time, but all you need to know for now is that I plan to rule this universe forever ... and for that I need *you*. So, you must allow General Kurg to bring you to me."

"Not a chance! If you want me you'll have to come and get me yourself," cried Frog.

"Oh no ... you'll not catch me setting foot on some alien planet," King Kroak began, wagging his finger. "All that *dust*. Come on, you must have noticed ... millions upon millions of tiny little particles, floating around, getting into your noseholes ... being all ... dusty. I prefer to do my conquering from a distance."

"You're bonkers," said Frog. "And I'm not going anywhere!"

King Kroak took a deep breath and then rolled his neck until it cracked.

"*Fine*. I'll come to you." The King's expression hardened. "But when I get there, I'm going to blow that world of yours into a million dusty pieces, right in front of your face."

The King pointed towards the sky as the world turned to shadow. At first Frog thought the sky was falling, but then he realized it was a ship – a vast saucer-shaped spaceship, hundreds, perhaps thousands of times bigger than any traceship Frog had ever seen. A city in the sky.

"What the—" Frog began.

"Look to the skies, Frog! I'm coming for you!" cried King Kroak.

With that, he shoved Frog off the top of the tower.

"WUUuAAAAAAA—!"

The Rescue

"—AaAARGH!"

Frog sat up and opened his eyes. He was back in the real world – on the island in the Inbetween – and Sheriff Explosion was frantically bleating at him.

"Now – *ow!* – what?" groaned Frog, rubbing a bump on his head. Not far from the wrecked house, Frog saw General Kurg, sunder-gun in hand once more, closing in on his friends.

"Go 'way, horrid ay'lun!" cried Princess Rainbow, stamping up and down.

Frog struggled to his feet but a rush of blood to the head sent him tumbling back to the ground. He saw his sunder-gun lying a few paces away and reached out for it – but

67

the general had already taken aim at Princess Rainbow.

"No!" uttered Frog. Then he felt something he hadn't felt for weeks.

A tingle in his toes.

"What the ... what?" he said.

KABOOM!

A bolt of lightning struck the traceship behind General Kurg. The ship exploded in a great fireball, sending shards of metal flying through the air. As black clouds gathered above them and rain began to pour, another bolt struck the ground between the general and Princess Rainbow.

"Kroak's teeth! It's happening again! The planet's turning on me!" cried General Kurg, stumbling back.

As more lightning streaked down from the sky, the general raced to the Inbetween, diving under the water to avoid the strikes. Frog looked up. Through the driving rain he saw something float down from the sky.

It was a large house, built from blue stone.

The Blue Howse

The blue howse is all sorts of magicul bisness. It used to belong to a wizard but he lost it in a game of cards. It can fly and has a magic door that leeds back to the royal palase by magic. The howse is our top-secret Headqwarters where we eat our lunch. It is also where we keep the sundur-guns we have ~~confisskated~~ ~~confisceited~~ stolen from the Kroakans.

"Man-Lor ... is saved?" said Man-Lor, as he and Kryl watched the blue house — otherwise known as the Omnium Gatherum — come to a rough landing on the island. The thunderstorm vanished as suddenly as it had arrived. A moment later the front door swung open.

"Did someone call for a dramatic rescue?" said a voice. From the doorway appeared Nigel, a barrel-chested bragon with rainbow-striped wings, a covering of dark red scales and an impressive plume of purple hair. He peered over a small pair of spectacles, adding, "Sorry it took us a while to get here — who would have thought there was an ocean all the way up in the sky? It was the rarewolf who followed your trail — and made all the thunder and lightning, by gosh!"

"Yes, well, there are *some* benefits to being an ancient god of the storms," grumbled the rarewolf, squeezing awkwardly through the door. The huge grey wolf was as tall as a horse, with curled tusks and eyes the size of plates.

"Rarewolf!" squealed Princess Rainbow, running over to him and hugging one of his legs. "I knew you'd save us! You're the most bestest pet I ever had!"

"Not this again…" sighed the rarewolf, not sure what to do with the princess's undying affection. "You do remember I'm the King and Queen's sworn enemy and that they slaughtered my entire race…"

"But you're *soooo* fluffy!" squeaked the princess, burying her face in his fur. "I'm going to cuddle you 'til you 'splode!"

The rarewolf groaned loudly. Frog, meanwhile, remained slumped on the ground, King Kroak's words still burning in his brain.

"I'm going to blow that world of yours into a million dusty pieces, right in front of your face."

"Frog, are you all right?" said Kryl gently.

"Look, I'm sorry I didn't tell you who I was before now. I—"

"Oh, so the truth is out at last," growled the rarewolf, trying to shake an adoring Princess Rainbow from his leg. "Well, good! If Frog is to fulfil his destiny and save the world, it's probably best he knows the full story."

"Leave him alone, beast," chided Kryl. "Can't you give your prophecy nonsense a rest for once?"

"Nonsense? The rarewolves' prophecy is an omen for our time!" growled the rarewolf. "You believe it, don't you, Frog?"

But Frog wasn't listening. He stared, motionless, at the wreckage of his home.

"None of it was real, was it?" he said, finally. "The island … Buttercup … my whole life was just made up to stop me from finding out I was supposed to end the world.

And now the world's ending anyway."

"But you said you'd stop it," said Princess Rainbow, crossing her arms. "I b'lieved you."

"Baa," added Sheriff Explosion, nudging Frog's leg with his nose.

Frog looked down at his trusty steed and sighed. Finally, he said, "King Kroak is coming. He's going to blow the world to pieces in one go."

"King Kroak is coming *here*? To Kingdomland?" gasped Kryl. "But ... why? When? How do you know?"

Frog thought about explaining that he'd *dared* his father to come to Kingdomland, thereby dooming the world to the worst of all fates ... but he thought it might not go down too well. And anyway, he'd been lied to his entire life. So instead he said, "I just know."

He held his arms wide apart. "And he's

got a spaceship this big ... except a million times bigger."

"Baa?" bleated Sheriff Explosion.

"The Farthership!" gasped Kryl, clamping her hand to her mouth.

"What's a Farthership, by gosh?" asked Nigel. Under his breath he added, "Nothing pleasant, knowing our luck."

"It's the most powerful ship in the fleet," replied Kryl. "Its *super* sunder-cannon can destroy an entire planet. If King Kroak is bringing the Farthership here ... we're doomed."

Frog stared across the wreckage of his house. Destruction followed the Kroakans wherever they went ... and it had to stop. Kingdomland was his home — and he wasn't going to sit about and wait for it to be destroyed.

"Doomed?" he said, clenching his fists. "Not if we defeat King Kroak, we're not."

The (New) Plan to Save the World

The inside of the blue house was just as blue as the outside. It was sparsely decorated with a blue table and chairs, and a simple blue stove and kiln for preparing food. Protruding from the floor by the window was a blue piloting lever, and in the middle of the room stood a blue door, which appeared to lead nowhere but was in fact an entirely magical route back to the royal palace of Kingdomland.

In fact, the only thing that wasn't blue was a huge pile of stolen Kroakan sunder-guns, stacked up in one corner of the room – spoils from the Defeat All Foes Team's various raids.

"We few versus a gigantic, planet-destroying

spaceship?" began Nigel, as the Defeat All Foes Team gathered round the blue table. "Doesn't sound like the odds are stacked in our favour, by gosh."

"Pfff — we've got odds coming out of our earholes," insisted Frog. "I may not have my top invincible sword but I've still got" — he rooted in his pocket and pulled out a carved stone talisman — "one last excellent magical!"

"Oh good," grunted the rarewolf. "It only took a few *hundred* of those to defeat ten traceships. We're saved."

"And that's not all! Look at all the gubbins we've pilfered!" added Frog, pointing to the pile of sunder-guns.

"Guns?" growled the rarewolf. "What use are guns if we have no army to fire them?"

"Could you at least *try* to be supportive?" huffed Kryl.

"Wait a miniature, the rarewolf's right!" cried Frog. "We should get our own army. All the proper champions have armies! This'll be great... I'll be the top army leader and skilled-up general. Nigel can be my second-best-in-command deputy, and—"

"I'm an ackshul princess – *I* should be second," protested Princess Rainbow. "No, wait, first."

"Sorry, Princess, this is serious business, not sparkly princess stuff," said Frog. "OK, from now on everyone should call me 'Green Leader' ... no, 'Boss Number One'... no, 'The Mighty Frog'!"

"I'll call you silly Greeny stupid head," cried the princess.

"Does it *really* matter who's called what?" growled the rarewolf.

"Five, six, seven..." continued Frog,

counting everyone in the room. "With my skills I probably count as two, so that's eight," he said. "How many do we need for an army?"

"Twelve at *least*," tutted Princess Rainbow, crossing her arms.

"Yoiks ... that's heaps," said Frog, rubbing his chin thoughtfully. "OK, the royal army is killed off or brain-slaved, so they're no good. Who else do we know?"

The Defeat All Foes team racked its brains. After a moment, everyone turned to Nigel (except Man-Lor, who was staring at his own elbow).

"Why are you all looking at me? I don't know any— Wait, the *bragons*?" Nigel blurted. "Impossible! We're not even on speaking terms since the Great Falling Out, truth be told. We tried to out-boast each other for twenty hours straight..."

"It's time to put your differences aside in the name of fighting a ginormous spaceship," said Frog.

Sheriff Explosion added an encouraging "baa".

Nigel sighed. "Very well, but don't blame me if they're no help at all. Bragons live to fly, not fight … and we're all cowards." He opened a drawer in the blue table and pulled out a small brass trumpet. "This is the Horn of Hotairia. With it I can summon my brothers and sisters from all corners of Kingdomland."

"How does it work?" asked Kryl.

"I'll show you," Nigel replied, taking off his spectacles dramatically. "But first I'll need to do what bragons do best — *brag*."

"I thought you only bragged so you could fill up with hot air and fly," said Frog.

"Ah, but sometimes you just have to blow

your own trumpet," explained Nigel.

The bragon's reedy voice became suddenly thunderous as he started to boast, awarding himself a long list of extraordinarily egotistical names. He bellowed them out in alphabetical order, from "Admiral Aceface Amazingstone" to "Zoom-balloon Zestypops". And with each boast, Nigel began to inflate, his barrel chest filling with hot air. Soon, he had swollen to more than twice his size, and begun to float towards the ceiling.

"Ready!" Nigel uttered, as Frog and Man-Lor grabbed a leg each to keep him grounded. "Cover your ears!"

With that, Nigel blew with all his might into the horn. He blew until his red face turned purple, until the sweat poured from his wings, until every last breath of air was blown out of his body. Then:

Toot!

"Huh... I thought it might sound a bit mighterier," whispered Frog, as Nigel caught his breath. "Now what?"

"With luck, the bragons will assemble at nightfall, atop the Cliffs of Resentment," puffed Nigel, replacing his spectacles. He paused for a moment, a grave expression upon his face. "Looks like I'd better start baking ... just in case."

"Baking?" repeated Frog, but Nigel was already making his way to the kitchen.

Frog twiddled his thumbs. Then he stared at the magical blue door leading back to the royal palace.

He rolled his neck until it cracked.

"Pfff — nightfall is *ages*. Who wants to help me get my sword back?"

"Saving my mummy and daddy is *tenty* times as important as getting a stupid sword," insisted Princess Rainbow. "Promise you'll rescue them! Promise!"

"Fine – if they're still at the palace, I'll bring them back," huffed Frog. "But only so they can make up numbers in the DAFT army."

"I'll come with you," said Kryl. "I have the kroak cloak, too. I can camouflage myself, or—"

"Or pretend to be someone else?" interrupted Frog, pointedly. After a moment, he shrugged and said, "Fine. You can help me carry the King. He's pretty heavy…"

As Frog and Kryl made their way over to the blue door, they activated the kroak cloak

— and disappeared. A moment later, the door opened … and closed behind them.

"*Please* bring back my mummy and daddy," said Princess Rainbow quietly. "And some treasure."

It had been almost an hour since Frog and Kryl had gone through the blue door. Man-Lor was piloting the Omnium Gatherum through the sky, since Nigel was still busy baking. Princess Rainbow, meanwhile, kept trying to plait the rarewolf's tail fur to make him look "extra-pretty".

"Princess used to plait Man-Lor's hair," Man-Lor sighed.

"Nigel, are you making plumberry pie for my surprise Princess Plumberry Pie Party?" asked the princess hopefully.

"If only, by gosh," muttered Nigel, sighing a long sigh. "I'm sorry to say that—"

"Blast it all!" interrupted the rarewolf, pacing up and down. "They've been gone too long! If that idiot Frog has gone and got himself killed, I'll ... I'll kill him!"

"Baa?" said Sheriff Explosion, waking from a nap.

"You need to b'lieve like you say you do, fluffy-wuff," Princess Rainbow replied, *klik-klak-ing* over to the blue door in her tiny heels. "Greeny promised he'd save Mummy and Daddy, and he promised he'd save the world. I b'lieve him! You should just b'lieve that everything is going to be good and it will be goo—"

KRROOM!

The blue door was blown open, turning it to splinters and flinging Princess Rainbow across the room.

"Everything is bad! Everything is *so* bad!" screamed a battered Frog, as he stumbled through the doorway — now little more than a stone frame — dragging an unconscious Kryl behind him. As Frog collapsed to the floor, sunder-beams streaked through the doorway, shattering windows and blasting great chunks off the walls.

"Gah!" cried Nigel, leaping for cover behind the stove. "What's happening, by gosh?"

"Kroakans everywhere!" Frog cried. He turned back to see dozens of Kroakan troopers racing from the palace towards the magical doorway, their sunder-guns blazing. More windows were shattered and the blue table obliterated as the Kroakans advanced.

"They'll overrun the house!" Nigel shrieked, as a sunder-beam burned a path through his hair plume. "If they don't destroy it first!"

"I'll ... defeat them," wheezed Frog, trying to get up. "Just give me a minute... I just need to get my mightiness back..."

"Too late for that!" growled the rarewolf. He made for the door as more sunder-beams scorched his fur. "Find something to block up the doorway! I'll buy you some time..."

"You can't fit through…" gasped Frog. "You already tried … your rump is too big!"

"Perhaps I just lacked the proper motivation," replied the rarewolf. "Now, for once, just do as I say!"

The rarewolf went to leave, then he turned back.

"Save the world, Frog," he added. "I believe in you."

"Wait!" cried Frog, but the rarewolf was already leaping at the doorway, forcing himself through the cracking stone with all his might. With a colossal effort he struggled to the other side. Frog heard him cry, "Let's see how you handle an enemy with teeth!" as he pounced on the Kroakans.

"Fluffy wuff!" Princess Rainbow squealed, as she and Frog struggled to their feet.

While Nigel tried to block up the doorway with chairs, they watched the rarewolf tear into the Kroakans with tooth and claw, tossing them like rag dolls or swatting them with his paws. At first he seemed to shrug off the searing sunder-beams, but the Kroakans kept coming at him, one after the other, their weapons blazing. Soon, the beams began to take their toll. The rarewolf cried out in pain.

"Rarewolf!" cried Frog and Princess Rainbow together, as the rarewolf slumped to the ground. He tried to get up, but was quickly buried beneath the Kroakan hordes.

"Hang on, rarewolf! I'm coming!" Frog cried, pushing past Nigel's feeble chair fortifications. He was about to step through the doorway when he felt a huge hand press on his chest. He looked up and saw Man-Lor staring back at him, shaking his head.

"This is job for Man-Lor," began the barbarian. "I am Man-Lor."

Man-Lor pushed Frog and the princess back towards Nigel, and then grasped the doorway in his massive hands. With an almighty heave, he wrenched it out of the floor. His great muscles strained as he carried it across the room, before kicking open the front door.

"The rarewolf is still in there!" squealed Princess Rainbow. "Stop, champ'un!"

But for the first time in his life, Man-Lor did not do as the princess commanded. With the last of his strength, he pushed the doorway out of the house. It toppled, spiralling through the air, and plummeted towards Kingdomland. Within seconds, it had disappeared into the clouds.

The Last of the Excellent Magicals

It was a few seconds before anyone in the blue house moved or spoke. Then Kryl awoke with a start and looked around at the devastation. "What happened? Where's the blue door? Where... Where's the rarewolf?"

"He ... he saved us," muttered Frog. "He went through the door to fight the Kroakans."

"He's ... gone?" asked Kryl.

"He wanted me to save the world," Frog added, "and I couldn't even save him."

"I command we go to the palace and get him back," sniffed Princess Rainbow, tears streaming down her face. "He was fluffy and smelled of rain, and I command we get him back!"

"Baa," added Sheriff Explosion sadly.

"I'm sorry, Princess, but we can't risk it," said Kryl, dragging herself to her feet. "We can't ever go back to the palace – it's overrun."

The princess wiped the tears from her eyes. "But what about Mummy and Daddy? I want my mummy and—"

"Yoiks, I forgot all about them!" Frog said, reaching into a pocket. "I hope they're not too squished…"

He pulled out a clenched fist and then opened his hand. Two tiny figures tumbled on to the floor. Though they were no bigger than beetles, the princess recognized them immediately.

"Mummy! Daddy!" she squealed. "You saved them!"

"Hail, Kroak!" squeaked the shrunken King and Queen in unison.

"Well, technically they're still evil brain-slaves … plus I had to use the last of the excellent magicals to shrink them to pocket-size…" Frog scratched his head. "But yep! I totally saved them!"

The King and Queen began attacking the princess's fingers and thumbs.

"They're cute like my pet glamsters!" said the princess, excitedly gathering up her parents. "I'll keep them in my princess pockets. Mummy always said I should have pets instead of friends."

"We'll find a way to fix them," assured Frog, though he had no idea how. "It's just a shame I didn't manage to find—"

"This?" said Kryl, limping over to him. From inside her robes she drew out a gleaming sword.

"Basil Rathbone!" cried Frog. "How did—?"

"I wrestled it from the Queen just before you shrunk her," replied Kryl, handing him the sword. "It cost me a good scratch, but it was worth it."

"I... Thank you," said Frog.

Kryl smiled. "You're welcome. If it goes some way to making amends, then..." She trailed off. Finally she added, "Frog, I want you to know I only did what I did because I am your Keeper. I made a vow to keep you safe. I have betrayed my people and my King to keep you—"

"Man-Lor was told to say when he sees cliffs," said Man-Lor, from the controls. He paused for a moment. "Man-Lor sees cliffs."

Nigel hurried over to one of the smashed windows, holding a freshly baked pie in his claws.

"The Cliffs of Resentment!" he cried, looking out. "We've arrived, by gosh!"

Frog, too, peered out. They had plunged back into the darkness of a ruined Kingdomland, but in the gloom he could make out a vast cliff face, jagged and unwelcoming, plunging into an icy ocean.

Man-Lor set the blue house down atop the cliff and the occupants of the Omnium Gatherum made their way outside.

"How do we know if the bragons *hearded* your teeny-weeny trumpet toot?" asked Princess Rainbow, peering up into the blackened sky.

"How do we know if they're coming?'

"Look up, by gosh," replied Nigel, staring at his pie as if it was his worst enemy. "And remember to cover your ears."

The Gathering of Bragons

Dozens of winged shapes emerged from the darkened sky, swooping and circling around the blue house. In moments, Frog and his friends were surrounded by bragons of all different colours, shapes and sizes. They plunged through the air to land on the clifftop.

"I still say we're wasting our time, by gosh," whispered Nigel, clutching his pie.

All forty-eight bragons glanced uneasily at each other, no one daring to speak. At last one of their number stepped forward. He stroked a long white beard and beat his silver wings dramatically.

"Good day to you, inferiors! It has been a long time since any of you have been intimidated by my eminence!" he boomed. "Who here committed the deed? Who blew their summoning horn?"

"Not I!" bellowed a smaller bragon, spreading her four wings to reveal a dazzling array of blue feathers. "I am far too wondrous and sure-footed to need help from any of you!"

"Nor I!" boomed another. "I have done my best to avoid you all, lest my handsomeness make you weep with jealousy!"

"What is that glorious fragrance?" cried

a third. "Why it's me, smelling better than all of you!"

"Pray silence for the Regent of the Remarkable!"

"Behold, the Duchess of the Undaunted!"

"Call me Lord Quentin the Insurmountable!"

Soon, their booming boasts were so loud that the cliffs began to crack and crumble.

Frog drew his mighty sword.

"Bragons!" he shouted at the top of his voice, Basil Rathbone flashing in the moonlight. "I am The Mighty Frog, skilled-up champion and— Hey! Shut up your faces! This is important stuff!"

But not even Princess Rainbow, who was standing right next to him, could hear Frog's cries.

"Hush! Bad *braggins!*" she squealed, putting her fingers in her ears at the sound of the bragons' boasts.

"They'll be filled up and flying off before you have a chance to be heard!" Kryl yelled, watching the bragons inflate. "We need to get their attention!"

"Should I blow something up? That usually helps!" shouted Frog, drawing his sunder-gun.

"No!" said Nigel. "There is only one way to stop a bragon bragging!"

"What did you say?" hollered Frog.

"I said, there's only one way to stop a bragon... Never mind!" Nigel yelled. He strode towards the boasting beasts until he was directly in front of the old, silver bragon. "I'd rather hoped it wouldn't come to this, by gosh," he added with a sigh. Then he took a deep breath ... and held out his pie. Suddenly, the bragons fell silent.

"What the ... what?" muttered Frog.

"Is ... is that what I think it is?" the silver bragon whispered at last.

"It's *humble pie!*" cried the blue-feathered bragon. "Don't—!"

But it was too late. Nigel closed his eyes, and shoved the pie into his mouth.

A gasp rang out from the bragons as they watched Nigel swallow the pie whole. There was a long moment of horrified anticipation, and then Nigel slowly opened his eyes. He looked down, patted his belly and breathed a long sigh of relief.

"You ... you ate humble pie!" muttered the silver bragon. "Why didn't you shrivel up like a raisin-berry?"

"What's 'humble pie'?" asked Frog.

"It's a bragon legend, by golly," explained the blue-feathered bragon. "It is said that if one bragon eats humble pie in front of another, he will shrivel and wither, never to inflate — never to *fly* — again! It is the most lowering thing a bragon can do."

"I never had reason to test the theory until now," said Nigel, picking pie out of his teeth. "But I knew it would be the only way to stop the bragons from boasting. It's funny what impending doom does to you, by gosh..."

"Baa," bleated Sheriff Explosion.

"Yoiks! Thanks, Nigel, that was risky business," said Frog. "I knew I made the right choice making you second-best-in command."

"I'm second!" cried the Princess. "I mean first! First!"

The Bragon Army

Having witnessed Nigel eat the humble pie all just to get their attention, the bragons became uncharacteristically modest – and thoroughly likeable. They reintroduced themselves using their real names and shared tea with acquaintances old and new (several of them having brought their own teapots along).

"Shall I pour?"

"You do it so well!"

"But *your* pouring is peerless!"

"No, yours!"

Before long, everyone had a cup of tea, Princess Rainbow was showing off her shrunken parents, and Frog was trying to work out who might make the best warriors in his army.

The Bragun Army: A Whoose Who

1) ~~NIJUL~~ ~~NIGUL~~ NIGEL
Maine Colour: Red and rainbow style
Skills: Eeting pie and not shrivuling.
Qwite fast. Good at baking. Nice.

2) OLD 'N' GRAHAM
Maine Colour: Grey
Skills: Sort of bragun leeder but does not look strong or
leedery. In fact smells like dust and looks like he mite
fall to peeses at any momunt.

3) SUSAN
Maine Colour: Blue like the blue
house but with more fethers.
Skills: Four wings, which meens she is
probubly three times as good at flying.
Speshul note: She is always staring at Nigel.
Maybe she is a spye.

4) THE YELLOW ONE WITH THE MAINE
5) THE PERPLE ONE
6) THE OTHER PERPLE ONE
7) I AM TOO BUSY SAVING THE
WORLD TO COWNT THE REST

Frog put away his diary as the old, silver-bearded bragon known as Old 'n' Graham hobbled forward.

"Nigel, for your willingness to wither like a lemon-lime left out in the sun, we, the bragons, most wondrous of all the creatures of Kingdomland — well, you know the rest — will hear your plea. So, tell us, why did you blow your horn and summon us?"

"I'm not sure where to start, truth be told," confessed Nigel. "I don't need to tell you that the whole world is ending..."

"I noticed that," replied Susan. "I remember looking outside and seeing the scorched earth and blackened sky and thinking, something's a little bit different today, and I couldn't quite put my claw on it, and then I thought, oh, don't overthink everything, Susan, you worry too much, and then I had a cup of tea and a dunky biscuit, and *then* I thought, I know what's different, by golly! The whole world is ending."

"I find everything is clearer with a nice cup of tea, by gosh," said Nigel, with a smile.

"Isn't it?" agreed Susan, blushing a deep blue. "Sometimes I think if I didn't have tea it would be the absolute end of the— You know."

"Perhaps after all this you and I could share a pot or two," said Nigel, adjusting his spectacles. "I mean, that is, if you'd like to—"

"Um, could we giddy this up a bit?" said Frog impatiently. "End of the World and all that…"

"Quite so – we should probably return to what we were doing before Nigel summoned us," Old 'n' Graham declared. "That is to say, hiding away with a nice cup of tea until all this blows over."

"'Blows over'?" interjected Frog. "Things are not going to blow over! They're going to blow *up!*"

"How awful," said Old 'n' Graham. "It sounds like you need an *army.*"

"You *are* the army!" Frog growled. "That's why we did the summoning! You're going to help us fight King Kroak."

"We, an army? Out of the question!" declared Old 'n' Graham. "Bragons fly, we do not fight. And we are cowards! Cowards with hollow boasts! Army indeed!" He turned to the bragons and spread his wings. "Bragons! We have been brought here under false pretences! This reunion is over."

"I told you this wouldn't work, by gosh," whispered Nigel, as the bragons prepared to leave.

"Baa," agreed Sheriff Explosion.

"It *has* to work," insisted Frog. "The bragons just need a motivating-leader speech from their top army leader and first-in-commanding general! Watch and learn. I'll—"

"No fair, you get to do all the speeching," complained Princess Rainbow. "I'm a princess so I do speeching all the time at home. I've speeched to my pets lots and they like it. They always go 'tweet!', 'meow!' and things."

"Pfff — it's not as easy as it looks," grumbled Frog. "It needs to be at least a million per cent inspirational."

"Silly Greeny," said the princess. She turned to the bragons and cleared her throat loudly.

"Hello, braggins, I am Princess Rainbow and I am a princess and I have three hundred and eleven — no, wait — three hundred and twelve dresses — and I like diamond puppies and newnicorns and strawbleflower cakes and my favourite colours are pink and another kind of pink and light blue not dark blue and my favourite smell is—"

"BRAGONS!" interrupted Frog, loudly. "What my fourth-in-command deputy is trying to say, is that we are about to face an enemy of such extreme badness that unless we defeat him, there won't be any place to hide and there won't be any tea to drink because this whole world will have been exploded into a million dusty pieces. But you can help us defeat King Kroak! We'll defeat him to bits, and when we do you'll all be given medals and champion badges and proper names like Baron Bopchops and Captain Smashbattle, and you'll have all the tea you can drink and heaps of people to listen to your braggings! And all you have to do is help me stop the badness! All you have to do is save your world! All you have to do is make a stand! All you have to do is *fight*! Who's with me?"

There was a long, awkward silence. The wind whistled around the cliffs. Then more silence.

"Anyone...?" he muttered.

"I will, by golly!" said a voice at last. Susan stepped out of the throng.

"As will I," declared another bragon, taking a stride towards them.

"And I!" said another.

Before long, forty-seven bragons had stepped forward. Only Old 'n' Graham remained.

"I knew I should have ignored that blasted horn," he huffed and took a single step forward. "Very well ... you have your army, Frog."

The bragons spread their wings and cheered in unison.

"My speech was still betterer…" tutted the princess.

As the newly formed army chanted his name, Frog grinned widely. Tomorrow he would defeat King Kroak, once and for all. He couldn't wait. He was The Mighty Frog, and nothing could stand in his way.

That night, Frog slept more soundly than ever.

The Incredibul Legend of Prince Krog

Chapter One

One upon a tyme there was King KROAK. He rooled over the planet Kroakas and also lodes of the universe. King Kroak had a spaceship as big as anything and he had one thowsand sons as well. Each son was sent to a diffrunt planet so they could conker it and be a mighty prince.

His best and most speshul son was called KROG. Krog was sent to a wurld called Kingdomland filled with magic and mistery and beauty and creetures of every description.

So Krog DISTROYED it.

He had bipods and traseships and sundur-guns and all sorts. It was all EXPLOOM! KA-SLAY! He made sure the hole wurld was all SCORCHED EARTH and BLACKUNED SKYS and CATASTROFEE!

I don't know what happuns next.

But I can't wait to find out.

The Inevitable Victory of Prince Krog

Krog replaced the top on his sunder-pen and closed his book. "Now for Chapter Two."

"What are you writing now, O Prince?" said a voice. From the throne in his royal traceship, Krog saw the hulking shape of General Kurg walking down the stairs towards him.

"It's a diary," he replied. "So my dad can see all the skilled-up conquering and world-ending I'm doing."

"By the Inevitable Victory! How could King Kroak be anything other than proud of you, Your Majesty?" cried General Kurg, placing a massive hand upon Krog's shoulder. "From the first wave to the second, you've been a *consummate* conqueror. You've scorched the earth, blackened the skies — total catastrophe!"

"Yep! No doubts on toast — I conquered this world to pieces," said Krog. He rubbed the back of his head. "I wonder how the other nine hundred and ninety-nine princes are doing with their worlds…"

"By the Right to Smite! I almost forgot — I rounded up the last of the native rebels so they can cower at your feet. Would you like the pleasure of brain-slaving them?"

"We did that yesterday — and the day before," said Krog. Then he hopped down from his throne with glee. "Let's do it again!"

Krog quickly adjusted his shiny black crown and cape, and raced out of the traceship. He emerged in the devastated remains of a once glorious palace of Kingdomland. Above him, the sky churned with black clouds and the comforting sounds of explosions could be heard from far and wide. In the centre of the courtyard, Kroakan troopers had surrounded a handful of kneeling prisoners.

"Yoiks, what's that smell? Oh, I know, it's the stink of defeat – and you all reek of it!" declared Krog, as he surveyed the rebels.

There was Princess Rainbow, daughter of the slain King and Queen of Kingdomland, her guardian, Man-Lor the barbarian, a crimson-scaled bragon by the name of Nigel, and a grubby-looking sheep.

Krog held out his hand and General Kurg passed him a handful of slave-nodes. "So, do you have anything to say before I void your brain space and load it up with slave juice?"

"You're a silly stupid-head and I hate you!" snapped Princess Rainbow. "You killed my mummy and daddy!"

"Actually, I just *ordered* them to be killed," Krog replied. "When you're a top prince like I am, conquering is mostly delegating. Mostly…"

Prince Krog threw one of the nodes, which stuck fast to the princess's forehead. Her eyes grew wide … and a moment later they turned inky black.

"Hail, Kroak," she said.

"Ka-SLAVE!" cried Prince Krog.

"Man-Lor begs for mercy," said the barbarian. "I am Man-Lor."

"Please spare me, by gosh!" added the winged creature.

"Woof!" said the sheep.

"Too late!" said Krog, throwing slave-nodes at each of their foreheads. Then he noticed a fifth prisoner, kneeling in the shadows. He was wearing a long black cloak, and his head was covered with a hood.

"It's slave o'clock, you rebel stink," Krog snarled. "Any last words?"

"Since you ask, yes," replied the hooded figure. "I'm *proud* of you."

"Begging won't save— Wait, what?" blurted Krog.

"I said I'm proud of you!" said the figure,

getting to his feet. Then he reached up and lowered his hood.

Krog's own face peered back at him.

"This is my kind of conquering!" said the figure.

Krog pressed his fingers to his temples. "What's going on?" he cried. "What... This isn't right... I'm supposed to... Oh *bumdrops!* Bumdrops to the moon times a million! I'm dreaming! This is all UNSLUMBER!"

"Well, *obviously*," sneered the figure. "I wasn't sure if you were ever going to work it out."

"I'm not Krog, I'm Frog ... Frog!" roared Frog, hammering the sides of his head with his fists. Then he looked up at the figure, his own face staring back at him. "And you're King Kroak!"

"What do you want, a prize? You should really be on top of this dream stuff by now," chuckled King Kroak. He pulled a black crown out of his cape and put it on his head. "I have to admit, though, all this does seem very real. I mean, look at you! *Prince Krog*, the mighty Kroakan prince, merciless conqueror of Kingdomland … just like you've always wanted."

"This isn't what I want!" Frog blurted. "I don't want to be a conquering anything and I don't want to be Prince Krog!"

"Are you sure?" scoffed King Kroak. "Look around, Frog … this is what you long for, even if you won't admit it. This is the world of your dreams."

Frog was about to speak, but for the first time in his life, he couldn't think of anything to say. He could see the prisoners, their minds enslaved, feel the heat from the scorched earth, smell the smoke from the blackened skies. It was as vivid as anything in the real world, and something about it felt ... *right*.

Finally, he said, "You told me I was different ... from your other sons. What did you mean? How am I—"

WHiiiiiiSHT – SHUNK!

"What the ... whAAAH!" Frog cried, glancing at King Kroak. The King had an arrow sticking out of his forehead.

"*Ow*," said King Kroak, giving the arrow a prod. "Looks like someone's trying to interrupt our UnSlumber party."

Frog followed the arrow's path to the top of a ruined tower. There stood Kryl, already drawing another arrow.

"Wake up, Frog!" she cried. "Your dreams have no hold over you! Don't let the King's lies poison you!"

"Lies?" howled King Kroak. "That's rich coming from you, Keeper! You've done nothing but lie to Frog since the day he hatched!"

Kryl said nothing. She unleashed another arrow, but this time King Kroak caught it in mid-flight, inches from his face. He glowered at the nearby Kroakan troopers.

"Has *anyone* noticed the traitor shooting arrows at the King?" he said. "Kill her!"

The troopers unleashed a volley of sunder-beams, destroying the tower and sending Kryl flying through the air. She landed hard on the ground, her arrows scattering in all directions.

"Kryl!" Frog yelled — but King Kroak was

already looming over her. He wrapped his fingers around her throat and hoisted her effortlessly into the air.

"I know what you're trying to do, Keeper," he began, squeezing her throat. "You think if you destroy me in the UnSlumber, I'll end up with my brain all stunk up in the real world. Arrow to the head and it's all over, am I right?"

"Wake … up … Frog…" Kryl wheezed.

"Stop…!" cried Frog. He raced towards King Kroak, but his limbs were slow and heavy, like he was moving through turnip soup.

"But there's one thing you didn't count on – I'm the mightiest of the mighty by a million. And do you know why?" King Kroak tugged the arrow out of his head. "BECAUSE I'M KING KROAK, STUPID!"

With that, he thrust the arrow into Kryl's chest. She gasped, once, and fell limp. King Kroak turned to Frog and winked.

"See you soon, son."

Frog was frozen to the spot. All he could do was cry out, "NOOOOOOOO—"

The Flight of Bragons

"—OOoOoo!"

Frog woke with such a start that he hopped to his feet. He was in the blue house, the smell of Nigel's freshly brewed pot of tea filling his nostrils. Princess Rainbow was making her shrunken parents ride Sheriff Explosion around the front room.

"Morning, sunshine!" said Nigel, pouring him a cup of tea. "You've been asleep for hours, by gosh — that marvellous speech must have taken it out of you."

"I... Kryl!" Frog began, scrambling to his feet. He raced to the other side of the room, where Kryl still slept, and lifted her into his arms. Her head fell limply to one side, her eyes rolling back.

"Wake up, Kryl!" he shouted, shaking her. "Please wake up…"

"Baa?" bleated Sheriff Explosion.

"What happened?" asked Princess Rainbow, returning her parents to her pocket. "Why is she so sleepy?"

"He did something to her brain in the UnSlumber," Frog replied. "He hurt her there and stunk up her brain in real life."

"'He'? Who's 'he'?" asked Nigel.

Frog didn't answer. He lay Kryl gently on the floor and stood up, his fists tightly clenched. "Tell the bragons to start boasting – we've got a long journey ahead of us. We're going back to the Inbetween."

Twenty minutes (and a lot of boasting) later, the Omnium Gatherum led the bragon army up through the clouds. While Nigel piloted the house, Princess Rainbow and

Man-Lor sat with Kryl. Frog, meanwhile, stared out of the smashed front window, the wind whistling around his head. The bragons soared alongside the house, filled to bursting with air, flying higher than they had ever flown.

"Baa," said Sheriff Explosion, nuzzling Frog's leg.

Frog ruffled the sheep's wool. "Don't worry, it'll be all right," said Frog, sounding less than convinced. His dream buzzed in his head like spiderflies. Did he really want to be a conqueror, deep down? Was there any point in being good, if he was destined to be evil? He was more confused than ever.

Frog took out his diary and chalk.

<u>Why you shud be GOOD</u>

1. You make more frends
2. Helping gives you a tingly feeling
3. People like you (except villuns and bad peeple)
4. Peeple give you top hero stuff like unbreakable sords
5. It is rite

Why you shud be BAD

1. You don't need frends
2. Distroying gives you a tingly feeling
3. You don't need peeple to like you because
   they are scaired of you
4. Villun clothes look better than hero clothes
5. It is fun

"Frog, if you don't mind me asking," said Nigel, "what *is* the plan to save the world from the titanic, world-destroying spaceship?"

The question shook Frog out of his musing. Nigel was right — he needed to focus on the matter in hand.

"The Inbetween is the plan," he replied. "The Inbetween is one hundred per cent magic, and Kroakan scanners can't see magic gubbins. That's why the rarewolf hid me there in the first place. So we wait on the island for the spaceship to arrive and then — *ka-trap!* — we attack before they spot us and *exploom* them all over the shop."

"Seems pretty watertight, by gosh," said Nigel, trying to sound positive. "What could possibly go wrong?"

Frog glanced over at the unmoving Kryl. Then he buried his doubts deep in the pit of his stomach.

The journey to the Inbetween was long, even by bragon standards. Some had to rest mid-flight, landing on the roof of the Omnium Gatherum and boasting themselves back to a sufficiently swollen state. By the time the flight of bragons passed over the top of the Inbetween and caught sight of the island, none of them had the energy to brag, even if they'd wanted to.

The blue house landed on the shore and

Frog, Princess Rainbow, Man-Lor and Sheriff Explosion stepped out, carrying armfuls of sunder-guns. They proceeded to distribute them among the bragons.

"How come they all get a *sundy-gun* and I don't?" asked Princess Rainbow, adding, "I want a pink one with sparkles on it."

"And that's why you don't get one," tutted Frog. "Defeating is serious business, not fluffy princess—"

A shadow fell across the island. There came a rumble in the air — a deep, grating hum that made every bone in Frog's body ache. He looked up. It was King Kroak's Farthership. And it was huge.

Frog's jaw fell open, and he felt his stomach turn.

"You're going to need a bigger gun," said Princess Rainbow.

The Farthership

The Farthership descended through the air. It was impossibly vast, as if the sky itself were falling slowly upon them. The oil-black spaceship glinted in the afternoon sun, its slick surface dotted with hundreds of blinking green lights.

"Baa…?" bleated Sheriff Explosion.

"They don't see us," said Frog. "The Inbetween's magic is working its magic!" He glanced over at the bragons, who were frozen with fear. Princess Rainbow, Man-Lor and Nigel, too, were rooted to the spot.

"It's really, *really* big," said Princess Rainbow. She took the shrunken King and Queen out of her dress pocket and lifted them up. "It must look even bigger for you."

"Hail, Kroak," squeaked the tiny brain-slaves.

"Bragons, start your boasting!" Frog commanded. "Boast the most!"

"I… I am the Duke… I am the g-greatest of the greatest of the great…" began Nigel, leading the way, and though his boasts seemed more hollow than ever, he started to fill with hot air. The other bragons joined in and were soon as swollen as their terror would allow.

Frog turned to Princess Rainbow. "Princess, you and Man-Lor stay in the blue house, where it's safe," he said. "I need you to look after Kryl and make sure no one stinks her brain up any more, OK?"

"But I want to do defeating!" she protested.

"Yep, well, you're five years old, so you don't get to fight in battles," replied Frog.

"You're *one* years old!" she snapped. "You're a baby!"

"Look, just stay in the house!" ordered Frog. "I mean it!"

"Man-Lor is happy to stay," confessed Man-Lor. "I am Man-Lor."

Frog leaped on to Nigel's back. Then he heard a "Baa?" and looked down to see Sheriff Explosion peering up at him.

"Sorry, Sheriff, you'll have to sit this one out, too," he said. "Hold on to the fort, I'll be back before you know it."

"Baa," bleated the sheep meekly.

Frog looked up into the sky. He checked his sunder-gun, patted the hilt of his sword and took a long, deep breath.

"This is it!" he cried. "Up, up and off we go!"

The air was filled with the sound of beating wings. Dust flew into the air as the bragons launched themselves towards the Farthership.

Frog drew Basil Rathbone and held it aloft.

"Bragons! Tomorrow we dine on polished sandwiches and roseberry wine!" he roared. "But today we don't eat until we defeat!"

The Battle Begins

"They still haven't noticed us!" cried Nigel, as he flew towards the gleaming hull of the Farthership, Frog riding upon his back. "It's looking good, by gosh!"

"Bragons! Take aim!" shouted Frog, as they came within firing distance. "And make sure you've got the shooty end of your guns pointed at the ship!"

"For Kingdomland!" cried Susan.

"For our continued survival!" added Old 'n' Graham.

"For... Actually, I think that covers it," added Nigel.

"Fire!" Frog yelled. The bragons opened fire and their sunder-beams streaked through the air, battering and scoring the Farthership's hull. The bragons soared along the underside of the ship as fire and sparks spewed from gashes in the hull.

"Do your thing, Basil Rathbone!" Frog jammed his invincible sword into the hull, slicing through the metal like it was turnip soup. More sparks spat out from inside as Nigel swooped away.

"And that's how you bring the mightiness!" Frog cried. He glanced back and caught sight of movement along the rim of the Farthership's hull. Black saucers, ten or more of them, darting through the air towards the bragons.

"King Kroak's got his own traceships!" Frog cried. "Bumdrops!"

"Bragons, beware, by gosh!" shouted Nigel.

The bragons barely had time to wheel around as the traceships' sunder-beams lit up the sky.

The agile bragons ducked and weaved as best they could, but they weren't all fast enough. In the first volley, six bragons fell from the sky and plunged down into the Inbetween.

"Yoiks..." uttered Frog, as he watched the bodies fall. "Everyone – split up! Stay close to the Farthership!"

The bragon army scattered, spiralling in every direction, swooping up and over the top of the Farthership, frantically boasting to maintain the right level of inflation.

"Here they come again, by golly!" yelled Susan. Frog looked back. The traceships had pursued them over the top of the hull.

"They're gaining on us!" cried Old 'n' Graham. "We're doomed!"

"Doomed shmoomed! Just be ready with your sunder-guns – I'm going to distract them with my skills!" cried Frog. "Nigel, slow down! Let the traceships catch us up!"

"*Catch us up?* Oh poo," sighed Nigel. He tucked in his wings and let out an almighty burp. Susan and Old 'n' Graham glanced back as Nigel halted in mid-air.

"Perfect," grinned Frog, as the traceships soared over his head. With that, he pushed off Nigel's back with his mighty legs – and launched himself into the air.

"WHUF!" he cried, landing atop one of the traceships with a thud. He bounced and skittered along the ship's surface, digging his sword into the metal and gouging a great hole out of the hull. Then he drew his sunder-gun and blasted the exposed machinery within.

"Eat the defeat! EAT it!" he roared. "I am The Mighty Frog!"

Explosions rocked the traceship and it listed in the air, smoke and fire spewing out from inside. As it careered out of control, Frog leaped on to another traceship, plunging Basil Rathbone's blade into the hull. He gouged and blasted again, before an almighty hop carried him on to a third. As he hacked and blasted wildly, the other traceships broke off their attack.

"Nigel!" cried Susan, as the bragon army regrouped. "Now's our chance, by golly!"

"Then fire!" Nigel declared. "Fire! Fire!"

And fire the bragons did. Within moments, the remaining traceships were sent crashing on to the Farthership's surface or plummeting into the Inbetween.

"I'll smash you to bits and pieces!" Frog

roared, slashing away at the final traceship.

The panicked pilot flew his burning ship high into the air, looping and whirling to shake off its determined passenger. Frog dug in his sword and held on.

"Frog!" cried Nigel, pursuing the trail of smoke and fire into the sky. "Jump, by gosh! The ship is going to—"

BOOM!

The Tide Turns

As the traceship exploded in mid-air, Frog found himself plummeting through the sky, his armour scorched and burning.

"Yoooooooiiiiiiks!" he cried. In his daze he spotted the Farthership below him. He closed his eyes and braced himself for a rough landing...

"Got you, by gosh!" Nigel shrieked, as he grabbed Frog in his claws. "Next time, warn me you're going to do something reckless! Or perhaps I should just expect it..."

"Just — *ow!* — just get us back into the battle!" yelled Frog. He saw smoke pouring from the Farthership's damaged hull as the bragons swooped around it, sunder-guns blasting. "We're doing it ... we're defeating the bumbles out of—"

There came a sudden noise — a deep, growling whirr, emanating from inside the Farthership. Then Frog saw a hundred portholes slide open along the rim of the ship … and a hundred sunder-cannons emerge from inside.

"Yoiks!" cried Frog. "Move! Everyone—"

Frog's cries were drowned out by the sunder-beams' shrieks. The sky-filling barrage blasted out in every direction. The bragons ducked and dived but most could not avoid the bombardment. They fell one after the other, like spiderflies being swatted out of the air.

"No!" Frog cried.

He saw a wounded Old 'n' Graham crash on to the surface of the Farthership. Then, as Susan dived after him, she, too, was hit.

She spiralled through the air, her wings aflame.

"Susan!" howled Nigel. "Hold on! I'm coming, by gosh!"

Nigel dived towards her, weaving to avoid the blasts – but a sunder-beam struck him a glancing blow to the head. Frog clung on as Nigel spun helplessly through the air.

"AaaaAAAAAaaa—"

KRUDD!

Frog clambered painfully to his feet. The glinting black hull of the Farthership seemed to go on forever. He could see flashes of colour dotted all about – the bodies of injured bragons. He spun around to see Nigel lying a few paces away, his wounds still smoking.

"Nigel!" Frog cried, limping over to him. "Get up! We have to get you out of here!"

"All out of air ... truth be told," the

bragon whimpered through the cacophony of sunder-beams. "Go... They're coming..."

Frog turned and saw a dozen Kroakan troopers racing across the surface of the ship towards them. He drew his sword.

"I'm not going anywhere!" he screamed, as the Kroakans surrounded them. "I'll take you all on!"

"I'm afraid that's not an option, Your Majesty," said the foremost Kroakan. She was tall and muscular, with distinctive horns above her eyes and striped green skin. "King Kroak has ordered us to bring you in alive and unharmed."

"Tell King Kroak to stuff his head in his armpit and sniff it!" roared Frog.

"How vivid," the Kroakan noted. "Let us try again — my name is Major Krung, and I give you two choices. One, surrender with immediate effect — and your army is free to leave. Or two, maintain your defiance, and watch this creature — watch all these creatures — perish."

"Run ... Frog..." wheezed Nigel. "They'll blow up ... the world ... anyway..."

"I..." said Frog. The shriek of sunder-beams rung in his ears.

"Last chance, Your Majesty," said Major Krung. She aimed her sunder-gun at Nigel's head.

"Wait!" Frog cried. "I... I surrender."

"One more time, my Prince," said Major Krung, cupping her hand to her earhole. "The roar of battle and all that..."

"I surrender!" cried Frog. "I surrender!"

"I thought that's what you said," said Major Krung. With that, she swung the butt of her sunder-gun into Frog's head, and he fell unconscious to the floor.

The King's Happy Place

Frog opened his eyes. He found himself floating helplessly in the void of outer space, an endless ocean of blackness speckled with stars and planets.

"Not *again* … this is the UnSlumber, as sure as turnips are turnips!" he groaned. "Well, you may as well wake me up now, King Kroak! 'Cause whatever it is you want to blah on about, I don't want to hear it!"

"Ah, but this is different," said a voice. King Kroak floated past, clad in his familiar black cloak and crown. "This isn't *your* UnSlumber, Frog. It's mine."

"I don't care!" Frog snarled. "Are the bragons all right? You said you'd let them go!"

"Who, those flying whatsits?" said King Kroak, spinning upside down. "I let them run off to lick their wounds. They'll be fine … until I blow up this world, of course."

"That's not going to happen!" barked Frog. "I'm going to defeat your face in!"

"Pfff – didn't you just surrender?" scoffed King Kroak. "Anyway, the reason I brought you into *my* UnSlumber is because I want to show you all this – my happy place!" He waved his arm across the vastness of space, dotted with planets. "You see these worlds? I've conquered them all!"

"I'm not talking to you, so shut up," insisted Frog.

"You'll get nowhere with that attitude, young man," said King Kroak. He reached out a hand for a distant planet and plucked it from space, like taking fruit from a tree.

He held the world in his hand. "You see this? This is Kroakworld Four Zero Six. And I want you to have it!"

Frog squealed as King Kroak tossed the planet towards him.

"Yoiks! Careful with that!" Frog cried, just managing to catch it in his right hand.

"Have this one, too!" The King plucked another planet from space and pitched it to Frog. Then he grabbed yet more planets from their orbits and tossed them at Frog. "And this one! And this! And this red one!"

"Stop!" Frog howled, by now juggling an armful of worlds.

"And not just those," King Kroak said with a smile. "Right now, there are a thousand new worlds falling to the Kroakan Empire. A whole *universe* of worlds. And, in time, I want you to have them all."

"I don't want them!" barked Frog.

"Yes, you do! Don't forget I've seen your dreams, Frog!" laughed King Kroak. "You can't fight your destiny…"

"I'm not like you!" roared Frog. He tried to get away, kicking out with mighty legs, but there was nothing to push against.

"Hey, here's a big one!" cried King Kroak, grabbing a planet twice as big as any other. "Why, it's Kroakas itself – the royal home world! And it's all yours!"

With that, King Kroak threw the planet as hard as he could at Frog's head.

"Hey! Don't—"

BUNK!

The Real King Kroak

"OW!"

Frog sat up. He was on a high bed in an almost luminous white room. He was dressed in a new suit of bright white Kroakan armour, that fitted him like a glove and smelled of fresh laundry.

"What the ... what?" Frog mumbled. He spotted a small circular window in the wall and peered out. Far below he could see the Inbetween, glistening silver. "Where am I? This had better not be more UnSlumber, I'm sick of all that real or not real bumdrops!"

"I can assure you, the Farthership is *very* real," said a voice.

At the far end of the room the doorway was open. Major Krung was flanked by two troopers. They were all dressed in bright white versions of their Kroakan armour. The major was holding Basil Rathbone. She held out the sword to Frog. "Here you are. Your weapon has been *decontaminated* . . . as have you. King Kroak is very particular about foreign particles."

"Is it true?" Frog began, taking his sword. "Did King Kroak let the bragons go?"

"They're safe . . . for now," Major Krung replied. "Please come with me."

The major led Frog through gleaming white corridors, one after the other. Finally they stopped outside a circular door, which slid open.

"After you, my Prince," said the major. "And welcome to your destiny."

Frog stepped inside. He found himself inside a bright, white chamber, bigger than any room in the royal palace. A window occupied the entire far wall, looking out over

the sky. And facing the window was a great white throne.

"Welcome to my humble home-stroke-world-destroying spaceship," said a voice.

The throne turned slowly, until it faced Frog. Upon it sat a figure dressed in a bright white cloak with a hood covering his face.

"King Kroak..." said Frog.

"We meet at last. Show yourself!"

King Kroak reached two woolly hooves up to his head and lowered his hood. Frog's eyes grew wide.

His trusty steed stared back at him.

"*Sheriff Explosion?*" Frog shrieked. "It's not... You're not... It can't be!"

"Baa!" bleated the sheep.

"*You're* King Kroak?" Frog blurted, his head spinning. "What the bumbles is—"

"Baa! Baahahaha!" The sheep seemed to burst into laughter as a shimmering haze engulfed him. As the haze cleared, Frog's mouth fell open. The real King Kroak stood before him. He was immense – a towering titan, taller than any Kroakan Frog had ever seen. The King's skin was a bright mottled green, with two long antennae protruding from his forehead, and in place of his robes he wore a spotless suit of white armour.

"Why the long face, Frog? Can't you take a kroak-cloak joke?" laughed King Kroak, his voice booming and resonant.

"You're horrible like turnips!" said Frog, drawing Basil Rathbone. "Here comes the defeat!"

The King loomed over him.

"Have you ever wondered *why* you like defeating things so much?" he asked. He strode to the window, in great, assured steps.

"Because right after defeat comes *conquest*. It's time to face up to who you are, Frog. Let's start by getting to know the family…"

King Kroak waved his hand, and the window behind him became a view-screen. Upon it were countless Kroakan faces, each slightly different from the other, but none a day older than Frog.

"Meet your brothers," said King Kroak. "All nine hundred and ninety-nine of them!"

"They're my brothers?" blurted Frog, peering at the screen.

"Yep! And no two are alike," laughed the King, pointing to one of the faces. "Karg here is always conquering outdoors, while Klorr over here likes to plan his conquests from the comfort of his ship... Krorg loves blowing things to pieces, while Kane is all about brain-slaving. And while they're all merciless conquerors, in their own way, none of them are ... *me*. None of them will ever rule as well as I rule or conquer as well as I conquer or be as hands-down, full-on awe-mazing as I am."

Before Frog could muster a "Pfff", King Kroak added, "That's the problem with being King — eventually someone has to take your place. But then it hit me! What if I could find a way to rule forever?" The King waved his hand, and the images of his nine hundred and ninety-nine sons faded to be replaced with a view of the afternoon sky. "So I found a way to *replicate* myself."

"Replicate…?" repeated Frog, not sure what he meant.

"You are more than my son, Frog… You're me. You're my exact *clone*," said the King with a grin. "You are King Kroak, reborn!"

The Green Button

Frog couldn't move. The King's words had frozen him to the spot.

"Didn't you hear me?" said King Kroak. "We are identical in every way. You're my perfect copy ... my duplicate... You're me!"

"But... But I can't be you," Frog said, the colour draining from his cheeks. "I don't want to be you! You're all the badness in the universe, plus a million!"

"It's your destiny!" the King cried, his fists clenched. He took a deep breath and composed himself. "Look, son, I only sent you to this dust-riddled planet because I wanted to give you a chance to have a *normal* childhood — a chance to do kid's stuff, like conquering your own planet and bringing about the End of the World! I didn't even tell your Keeper or General Kurg who you really were — I thought it would be nice to break the news myself, father to clone!"

"No... I'm not you..." muttered Frog weakly. But he was, and he knew it. He stared into King Kroak's eyes and saw his own eyes staring back at him. Had he not felt as if his world had just ended, Frog might have been pleased about how mighty he was going to look as a grown-up.

"I almost forgot!" cried King Kroak. He reached into his pocket and took out a small cube with a round green button set into one side. "See this? This is the Green Button. I love buttons, especially ones that make noises. *Boop beep boop!* Well, this one is specially encoded to work *only* when I press it.

But since you're me, it also works if you press it! Nifty, eh?"

"What does it do?" said Frog, already dreading the answer.

"Oh, nothing much … it just FIRES THE SUPER SUNDER-CANNON! Imagine a gigantically enormous version of a normal sunder-cannon that blasts a super sunder-beam straight into the core of the planet. Instant chain reaction — no more world! Heaps of fun!" The King's finger hovered over the button. "So, do you want to press it or shall I?"

"Don't!" Frog cried.

"What's wrong with you?" said King Kroak. "I've just told you, you're the future ruler of the universe and you're acting like I got dust in your boots!"

"You can't destroy the world! I won't let you!" Frog growled.

King Kroak shook his head. He thought for a moment, tapping his fingers against his chin.

"OK, *fine* … I'll make you a deal," he began. "I'll spare this planet, since you seem to give so many hoots about it. I'll leave it alone forever. All you have to do is join me."

"Join you?" repeated Frog.

"Return with me to Kroakas. Take your place at my side and fulfil your destiny. We can conquer the universe together, father-son style," the King replied. "But — and here's the important bit — if you defy me at any point, then I shall return to this planet and wipe it off the face of existence. So, what do you say?"

Frog stared at the Green Button. His choice seemed like no choice at all — doom Kingdomland, or doom the rest of the universe — trillions of lives … maybe even hundreds. But then, wasn't that his destiny?

"I... I..." he began.

"Take your time, it's a big decision," said King Kroak. "But remember, whatever you choose, whatever you decide, what— The ... *what?*"

Frog looked up and saw King Kroak peering out of the window. He turned, slowly.

The blue house was flying towards them at high speed.

The Princess is Five and Three Quarters

"Is that … a flying blue house?" muttered King Kroak, as the Omnium Gatherum loomed large in the window.

"It's not showing up on my scanners!" cried Major Krung, checking a control screen on the wall. "It could be a trick…"

"*That* is no trick!" boomed King Kroak. "Move, it's going to—"

KRASSSSH!

The blue house smashed through the window! Frog leaped out of the way as it ploughed into King Kroak, flattening him and sending the Green Button flying through the air. Chunks of blue stone flew in all directions as the house spun and careened across the throne room until, finally, it slammed into Major Krung and her troopers and ground to a halt.

"What the bumbles...?" coughed Frog, struggling to his feet. As the dust cleared, the front door of the house fell open...

"*Princess Rainbow?*" Frog cried, as the princess stumbled out. He leaped over to her in two mighty hops. "What are you doing here?"

"I'm helping!" the princess replied happily. "You said I couldn't help because I'm only five but then I remembered I'm five *and three quarters*, so I can do what I want. And look! I saved you!"

"You're *bonkers*, Princess ... in a good way," admitted Frog, peering at the wreckage of the blue house in disbelief. "Wait, Kryl was in there! Did you—?"

"Silly Greeny," she tutted, brushing dust off her dress. "I told Man-Lor to take her outside for *freshed air* and then I flew the house by my own self. I checked and made sure it was empty. I'm not *shtoopid...*"

"Baa..." came a sound from inside the house.

"I meant *nearly* empty," Princess Rainbow added.

"Sheriff Explosion!" Frog cried, as the sheep raced out of the house, bleating in terror. "My trusty steed can never stay away from the action! He'll always find a way to my side!"

"Baa…" sighed the sheep. Frog glanced at the floor and spotted something among the rubble.

"The Green Button!" he said. He picked it up and dusted it off. "Come on, Princess, let's get this as far away from—"

KROOM!

Blue stone flew in all directions as King Kroak burst through a wall of the blue house with an almighty roar.

"Look at this DUST! It'll take forever to decontaminate!" he roared, frantically patting himself down. He stared across the room, fixing his stare upon Princess Rainbow. "You! You did this!"

"Leave her alone!" Frog cried, drawing his sword.

"Oh, so you're siding with the dust-bringing natives over me?" King Kroak snarled. "Fine! You had your chance! I'm going to blow your precious world to a million— Wait. *Where's* my Green Button?"

King Kroak checked his pockets, but the button was gone. He began shovelling rubble aside. "Where *is* it?"

"Looking for this?" said Frog, holding up the button with a self-satisfied grin.

"Give Daddy his Green Button," the King snarled. "NOW."

"Time to run, Princess!" said Frog.

Frog, Princess Rainbow and Sheriff

Explosion darted out of the door. The King roared in anger, bounding across the throne room and pursuing them into the corridor.

A moment later, a dazed Major Krung clambered out of the rubble of the blue house.

"King Kroak? Your Majesty, wait!" she began. She was about to follow, when a hand emerged from the wreckage. Major Krung grabbed it and pulled as hard as she could. The massive shape of General Kurg appeared, battered and caked in blue dust.

"What on Kroakas?" began Major Krung.

"Frog..." the general growled, his voice rumbling like thunder. *"Where is Frog?"*

The Bumdrops

"Run, Princess!" cried Frog, clutching the Green Button tightly as he, Princess Rainbow and Sheriff Explosion raced down a white corridor. "We have to get *this* as far away from King Kroak as possible! If he gets his hands on it he'll … he'll…"

Frog skidded to a sudden halt.

"What are you doing?" said Princess Rainbow. "I thought we were running away."

"Baa!" concurred Sheriff Explosion.

"You need to take this," Frog said. He held out the Green Button to the princess. "I can't be trusted with it."

"What are you on about, silly Greeny?" asked the princess.

"You have to take it, or I'll press it and

blow up the world," Frog explained. "It turns out I'm King Kroak's cloned-up self. We're the same down to our left nostril. I'm all the badness there is, plus a million, and there's nothing I can do about it."

"Baa," bleated Sheriff Explosion.

"Pfff ... that's the *bumdrops*," said Princess Rainbow, folding her arms. "You've had all sorts of chances to be bad. When the ay'lun invaders came it would have been easy-peasy for you to join up with them, but you didn't. You saved us instead."

"But—" Frog began.

"And *then* when they came back you saved us again. *And* you saved my mummy and daddy ... sort of," the princess continued, peeking into her pocket.

"Hail, Kroak," squeaked the King and Queen together.

"But that's not who I am really," said Frog quietly. "Deep down, I'm one hundred per cent merciless conqueror."

Princess Rainbow thought for a long moment, puckering her lips and squinting her eyes.

"What if you're not the him he is?" she said at last. "What if you're the him he would have been if he didn't have to be one hundred per cent *mers'less conker*?"

"Huh," said Frog, staring at the Green Button in his hand. "I never thought of that."

"FROG!"

Frog spun around. At the other end of the corridor stood King Kroak, his massive fists clenched.

"I've changed my mind about you, Frog!" he roared. "I think I'd prefer you dead, after all!"

The Super Sunder-Cannon

As King Kroak leaped towards them, Frog spotted a door to his left and dragged Princess Rainbow inside.

"Frog!" boomed King Kroak. "You are in *so* much trouble, young man!"

"Baa!" said Sheriff Explosion, scurrying in as Frog shut the door behind them.

Frog slashed at the door controls, sending sparks flying into the air. They ran down a zigzagging stairwell, descending into the machinery of the ship.

"Greeny! This way!" cried Princess Rainbow, spotting a narrow, red-lit corridor. They raced down it until they reached another door. Frog slashed it open and they hurried inside…

"Yoiks…" muttered Frog. They were in a vast, deep chamber. It plunged down and down like a bottomless pit. A spider's web of metal walkways crisscrossed the chamber and disappeared into the darkness. And descending through the chamber's centre was a huge metal cylinder – a sunder-cannon, bigger than a hundred blue houses.

"The *super* sunder-cannon!" said Frog in awe. He gripped the Green Button tightly in his left hand. "That's how King Kroak's going to blow up Kingdomland unless we—"

"Frog!"

Frog looked back and saw King Kroak in the doorway.

"Oh no – after the way you've behaved, you do *not* get to play with Daddy's doomsday weapon," he snapped. "Now give me the Green Button!"

"Psst — don't give him the Green Button," whispered Princess Rainbow.

"Well, *obviously*," tutted Frog, gripping the button tighter. Then he scooped Princess Rainbow and Sheriff Explosion into his arms and leaped down into the chamber.

"Yeeee!" cried the princess (drowning out Sheriff Explosion's terrified "Baa!") as they plummeted through the air. Frog began descending the chamber in mighty hops, leaping down from walkway to walkway.

"Bad clone! Get back here!" cried King Kroak.

Frog was mid-leap when he felt the King's boot slam hard into his back. He landed roughly on a walkway, sending Princess Rainbow and Sheriff Explosion skittering along it.

"Urf!"

"Eek!"

"Baa!"

As Frog scrambled to his feet, the King landed next to him with a *klung!* Frog drew his sword but King Kroak was already upon him. He grabbed Frog's arm and squeezed it like a vice.

"ARGH!" Frog cried, dropping Basil Rathbone on to the walkway.

Frog kicked out, landing both feet in King Kroak's face.

"That's it! You're grounded!" roared the

King, slamming Frog down to the floor with such force that it shook. By now Frog could see nothing but stars, but still he did not let the button go.

"Frog!" shouted Princess Rainbow. She raced towards King Kroak, hammering at his leg with her fists.

"Dusty thing! Get off me!" he growled, kicking her down the walkway.

"Princess…!" whimpered Frog feebly.

"It's such a shame when your child doesn't turn out like you'd hoped … but so much worse when they're your *exact* copy," sighed the King, turning back to Frog and plucking his sword from the floor. "So I'm going to teach you a lesson. First, I'm going to chop off your hand and take the Green Button. Then you're going to watch me destroy this dusty excuse for a planet."

"Stop, you..." whimpered Frog, with a last gasp of defiance.

"I could have given you everything you've ever dreamed of, Frog – I could have given you the universe!" the King cried. "Who wouldn't want that? Why couldn't you just be *me*, like you were destined to be?"

Frog opened his swollen eyes and peered up at King Kroak. Then he looked past him to Princess Rainbow, struggling to her feet.

"Because ... I'm not you," Frog wheezed. "I'm ... me."

"Weren't you listening? We're the same!" roared King Kroak.

"I know..." coughed Frog. "And maybe I did dream of being like you. Maybe I did want to be badness. But that just means I have to try harder ... *not* to be a merciless conqueror."

"That's loopy-doopy! Why would you try *not* to be something you already are?" asked the King.

"Because destiny ... is bumdrops," Frog wheezed. "Because my friend told me that if I'm you ... then that means you're me, too. And if things had been different ... then maybe *you* would have turned out like *me*."

King Kroak slowly raised himself to his full height, sword in hand.

"Huh," he said. "I never thought of that."

The Fatal Mistake
of General Kurg

"I never for a mikron imagined I could be anything but a merciless conqueror," said King Kroak, lowering Frog's sword.

"Didn't – *ow!* – didn't anyone ever ask you if you *wanted* to be a merciless conqueror?" Frog asked, sitting up.

"It never came up," replied the King with a shrug. "My life's always been about conquering. What else is there?"

Frog looked down at the Green Button in his hand.

"Well, *not* conquering," he suggested.

"Hmm…" the King said thoughtfully. He peered at Frog for a long moment. "But I've seen your dreams, Frog. Your inner conqueror, dying to get out…"

"Pfff — my inner conqueror gets beaten up every day by my inner *champion*," Frog replied. "My inner champion is extra skilled-up, heroic, good, quite handsome … and he always makes the right choice."

"Inner champion, eh?" mused King Kroak. "I don't think I have one…"

"You do," Frog replied with a smile. "He's me."

The King took a step back and rubbed his eyes. Frog looked up at Princess Rainbow, huddled together with Sheriff Explosion. He gave her a hopeful wink.

"But I can't just stop — I'm sort of in the middle of something," said King Kroak. "My army … this giant spaceship … the cannon that blows up worlds … only merciless conquerors have that stuff."

"You don't need that gubbins!" replied Frog. "You're the King. No one can make you be anything you don't want to be."

"But what if I *want* to be a merciless world-ending conqueror?" asked King Kroak.

Frog looked up at the super sunder-cannon. Then he got to his feet and rolled his neck until it cracked.

"Then I'll just have to defeat you," he said.

The King let out a booming laugh, which echoed through the vast chamber. He shook his head and looked down at Basil Rathbone. After a moment, he held it out to Frog.

"Take it," he began. "Before I change my mind and defeat *you* into next week."

"Pfff — I'd like to see you try," Frog tutted, taking the sword. He placed the Green Button carefully on the floor of the walkway. Then he gripped his sword in both hands.

"Not the Green Button," the King sighed. "It's my favourite…"

"No one should have the power to blow up an entire world," said Frog, and lifted his sword aloft.

"By the Void! Look out, O King!" came a cry. Frog and King Kroak glanced up. There, at the entrance to the chamber, sunder-gun in hand, was…

"*General Kurg?*" Frog blurted. "What the bumbles is he doing here?"

"I'll save you, Your Majesty!" the general cried, and took aim.

"Baa!" bleated Sheriff Explosion.

"Wait!" bellowed King Kroak. He whirled around to face General Kurg – but the general had already fired.

A green sunder-beam streaked across the chamber. Princess Rainbow ducked as it

flashed over her head. By the time Sheriff
Explosion had let out a panicked "Baa!" the
sunder-beam had found a target.

"Yoiks…" grunted King Kroak, his back
to Frog. Frog saw a look of horror on
Princess Rainbow's face.

"By the Twist of Fate!" howled the general, dropping his gun. "What have I done?"

"King Kroak...?" said Frog.

Slowly the King turned to face him. His eyes were wide and unblinking, his mouth half-open, and in the middle of his chest was a burning hole.

"Destiny..." he uttered – and fell on to the cold metal.

The Fallen King

"Somebody, help!" said Frog, kneeling over the fallen King.

"I was supposed to know … what the future held," coughed King Kroak, looking at the smoking wound in his chest. "How did I not see this coming?"

"You'll be all right," said Frog. "You're me … and I'm full-on mighty."

"Ugh," the King groaned, screwing up his face. "Would you at least get some of the *dust* off me?"

Frog gently brushed the dust off King Kroak's armour.

"Clean as whistles," Frog said.

"Your standards of cleanliness … are disturbingly low," the King tutted. "But maybe you're right ... maybe I could have been more like you. Maybe when I'm better ... I'll try doing that *thing* you were talking about. What did you ... call it again?"

"Um, being good?" replied Frog.

"Yep…" the King said with a cough. "That."

Frog heard King Kroak's final breath escape from his mouth. A moment later, he was gone.

Frog slumped to the floor. He wasn't sure what to feel. Until a minute ago, King Kroak had been his arch-enemy – but now it felt as if part of him was lost. Tears welled up in his eyes and he wiped them away with his arm.

"Frog!"

At Princess Rainbow's cry, Frog looked up to see Major Krung, General Kurg and a dozen Kroakan troopers leap down towards them. Frog plucked the Green Button from the floor just as Major Krung and General Kurg landed either side of him.

"Get away!" Frog cried. He struggled to his feet, brandishing his sword.

"My King! By the Turmoil, I'm sorry!" howled General Kurg, pushing Frog out of the way and collapsing to his knees in front of King Kroak. "I was just trying to complete my mission, Your Majesty! I stowed aboard that blue house-ship, in the hope that Frog would return... In the hope that I could deliver him to you as you commanded! Then I got locked in the toilet, but that's not important. *Then* I ended up here on the Farthership! I was just trying to complete my mission..."

The general's expression hardened. He stood up and turned to face Frog, his sunder-gun drawn.

"Frog!" he growled. "Just when I thought you couldn't possibly be more annoying, you make me shoot my own King! I'm going to finish you once and for all…"

"Bring it on!" Frog cried. "I'll defeat you to shreds!"

"I think not," said a voice. Major Krung drew her sunder-gun … and pointed it at General Kurg. "General, you are under arrest for the murder of King Kroak. Drop your weapon."

"What? But I was trying to… Prince Frog was… I'm a good and loyal…" he began, as troopers surrounded him. "By the Void, I'm going to be turned into protein bars, aren't I?"

As General Kurg dropped his gun and held his hands high, Frog tried to think of the best way to defeat the Kroakans, rescue the princess and save the world all over again. Major Krung took a step towards him. Then she replaced her sunder-gun in its holster, took a deep breath … and knelt before Frog.

"Prince Frog, by Royal Amendment Three Thousand and Forty-Nine of the Big Book of Kroakan Law, I hereby declare you the new King of Kroakas," she said. "Welcome to your destiny – Royal Majesty, Lord of All Planets, Rightful Ruler of the Universe … King Frog."

"What the … what?" said Frog.

The King Rises

On the island in the Inbetween, the surviving bragons had been tending to their wounded. They occasionally peered fearfully into the sky at the Farthership looming over them.

"Do you think they're still alive, by gosh?" said a bandaged Nigel, as he dressed the singed wings of Old 'n' Graham.

"Man-Lor is usually optimistic," said Man-Lor, refusing to take his eyes off the sleeping Kryl. "But Man-Lor thinks we're doomed."

"Nigel, look!" cried Susan, pointing up into the sky. "The Farthership is moving!"

"Bragons, to arms! Everyone on your feet, by gosh!" cried Nigel, grabbing his sunder-gun. "No more boasting ... we take our last stand here on this island!"

The Farthership descended slowly towards them, until its shadow plunged them into darkness. Just as it seemed the Farthership would squash them, it stopped dead. Suddenly a section of the hull slid open. Smoke poured out and a long, oil-black tongue snaked out from inside, forming a stairwell as it touched the ground.

"Here they come! Don't shoot 'til you see the yellows of their eyes!" Nigel cried, as the bragons' weapons trembled in their hands.

"Don't shoot at all!" cried a familiar voice. A moment later Frog emerged from the fog and limped down the steps, closely followed by Princess Rainbow and a bleating Sheriff Explosion.

"Frog! Princess! You're... How... Look out!" cried Nigel, as a dozen white-clad Kroakan troopers began descending the steps.

"It's OK," Frog assured them. "I ordered the Kroakans to make you all better with their super-science doctor gubbins. I get to order them around, you see, 'cause it turns out—"

"Frog is the King's *clone*?" came a cry.

General Kurg emerged from the Farthership in sunder-cuffs, led down the steps by Major Krung. "Why did no one tell me? I spent this entire invasion trying to destroy the heir to the Kroakan empire! I was doomed from the start! I was doomed to fail! I... I'm *doomed*."

As it turned out, Kroakan "super-science doctor gubbins" was far in advance of bragon medicine. The troopers bathed the bragons' injuries with strange green lights, which healed their wounds so quickly that anyone would think it was magic.

"So, you're King now, by gosh?" Nigel said, as Frog treated his singed wings. "But you were only gone an hour…"

"Being an ay'lun invader space King still isn't as good as being Princess of Kingdomland," insisted Princess Rainbow.

"Baa," said Sheriff Explosion, possibly in agreement.

"What are you complaining about, Princess?" Frog tutted. "They took the brain-slavery off your mum and dad and everything! Show Nigel!"

Princess Rainbow emptied her dress pocket, spilling her parents on to the ground.

"What's all this? Invaders everywhere! Sound the alarm!" squeaked the tiny Queen.

"Pop me back in your pocket, would you, Rainbow?" pleaded the King. "I was rather enjoying the peas and quiet…"

"They're the *cutestest!*" declared Princess Rainbow. "I'm going to make sure they stay teeny-weeny *forever.*"

The UnSlumber Loop

Before long, Frog's army of bragons were healed. But one patient did not recover.

"Why isn't she better?" said Frog, as he, Major Krung and the Defeat All Foes Team gathered around Kryl. She lay on the scorched earth, still and unmoving. Frog knelt down before her. "Why haven't you made her better?"

"I'm sorry, Your Majesty," Major Krung explained. "It is her *mind* that is broken. We have no remedy for that. Only the Keepers possess the power to enter the UnSlumber. Keepers and, of course, those of royal blood."

The major peered at Frog.

"Why are you staring at me?" Frog asked.

"Do I have something on my face? It's probably dust, I need to— Wait, you mean *me*? No way! I can't do all that UnSlumbering gubbins! I've never gone into anyone's dream business — not on purpose anyway. I wouldn't know where to start."

"Time is running out, Your Majesty," insisted Major Krung. "Your Keeper is fading fast."

"You can do it, Frog," said Princess Rainbow. "I b'lieve in you."

"Pfff — last time you said that, a lot of things got blown up," tutted Frog. He took Kryl's hand, closed his eyes, and tried to think UnSlumbering thoughts…

"Bumdrops! It's not working!" he snapped, opening his eyes. "I don't even know where to— Wuuhh?"

Frog found himself sitting cross-legged in

a large white room.

"What the ... what?" he blurted, leaping to his feet. "Yoiks... I'm doing it! I'm inside Kryl's dream! I'm actually UnSlumbering! Is there anything I can't do?"

Frog did a little dance to celebrate his success, before deciding it might be a good idea to look for Kryl.

He gazed around. The room was empty but for a lone figure standing at its far end, staring at a wide wall of shimmering gold.

"Kryl..." cried Frog, walking towards the figure. "Is that you?"

Kryl did not answer – it was as if she wasn't even aware of Frog's presence. Frog peered up at the wall and saw that it was not the wall itself that was gold; rather that it was pitted with a honeycomb of tubular holes. And filling each one was a shimmering golden egg.

"No way…" he said. "The golden eggs! These are my brothers, before they were born!"

Frog followed Kryl's gaze. She was staring at one of the eggs. Frog peered closer. There was something stamped upon its shell in Kroakan: SPAWN 5.1.3 (HANDLE WITH CARE).

"Is that… That's me! That's my egg!" he said. "This is where it all be— Yoiks!"

Suddenly Frog and Kryl were somewhere else entirely. The egg chamber had been replaced with the green-lit interior of a Kroakan spaceship. Frog glanced around to see Kryl watching General Kurg (and a host of other Kroakan troopers) clambering into large oval pods.

"Kroak's teeth! I hate *farsleep* – it always gives me nightmares," said General Kurg. "We'll see you on the other side of the universe, Keeper. Make sure Spawn Five One Three is trained and ready to conquer by the time he reawakens us."

"This is the farship that brought me to Kingdomland, isn't it?" asked Frog. He waved a hand in front of Kryl's face. "Kryl, wake up! This isn't real. This isn't—"

BOOM!

The impact of a mighty explosion rocked the farship. Frog glanced around and saw that Kryl's dream had changed again. General Kurg and the other Kroakans were already deep in farsleep, and Kryl was alone at the controls. Outside the view-screen Frog saw lightning bolts batter the ship. Frog quickly realized what was happening – Kryl was dreaming of the moment the rarewolf attacked the farship with lightning … the moment the farship crashed.

"We're going down!" Kryl cried in terror.

"It's just a dream, Kryl! Wake up!" cried Frog again, as the farship plummeted towards the gardens of the royal palace. "This is UnSlumber! It's not real! It's not—"

SPLOOOSH!

"BwUUuh!" cried Frog, as he burst out of ice-cold water. The dream had shifted again – he was now bobbing about in the royal lake, moments after the farship had crashed.

Kryl emerged beside him, her eyes frantically searching around.

"Kryl, listen to me! You have to wake up!" said Frog, blowing water out of his earholes. He caught sight of Princess Rainbow on the shores of the lake, plucking his golden egg out of the water. "King Kroak stunk your brain up! You need to—"

Frog's cries were drowned out by the sound of the rarewolf's savage roar. Everything had changed once more – he now found himself running down a corridor in the royal palace. Running not with Kryl, but Buttercup.

"Yoiks! This dream's moving pretty fast!" cried Frog, as he raced after Buttercup, the golden egg under her arm. "We're already at the bit where you run away from the palace! When the rarewolf attacked!"

Frog looked back to see the rarewolf doing battle with the Queen's Royal Guard. He tried to slow down – to slow the dream down – but he found himself running despite himself, as if caught up in its momentum…

"Kryl! Wait for me! Wait for me— AAAH!"

Frog felt his feet lift off the ground! Again, the dream had shifted – he was no longer in the palace, but rather being flung helplessly into the air, up and up in the middle of a tornado. Buttercup spun around him, clinging desperately to the golden egg.

Frog looked down to see Kingdomland, far below and quickly disappearing. After a moment he realized where – or rather when – they were.

"The rarewolf's sending us to the Inbetween!" he cried. "Kryl! Listen to me! This isn't real! Wake up!"

But still they flew higher and higher, until Frog saw the waters of the Inbetween, suspended in the air above him. They would hit it at any moment.

"Wake up!" Frog cried again. "Please—"

Frog found himself on the island on the Inbetween, and the dream began to move at a dizzying pace. He watched himself hatch from his own egg. Then he saw himself take his first steps … heard himself speak his first words … dizzying fragments of moments appeared and disappeared in an instant…

"Stop!" cried Frog, his head spinning. "Wake up, or I'm going to throw up all over your UnSlumber!"

But it didn't stop. Kryl's memories came ever faster... Frog saw the rarewolf plucking her from the island ... the first traceship attack ... fighting to escape the Kroakans at the royal palace ... faster and faster until Frog could no longer make sense of anything... Until suddenly he saw King Kroak holding Kryl by the neck – and thrusting her own arrow into her heart.

"Wuuh?" Frog sat up. He found himself sitting cross-legged in a large white room. There stood Kryl, motionless, staring at a shimmering gold wall.

He was back in the egg chamber.

"We're here again? What the bumbles…?" Frog grunted. "Is this what King Kroak did?

Sent Kryl's brain on a loopy-doopy loop? Some kind of rinse and repeat memory round and round? Well, bumdrops to that!"

Frog strode over to Kryl, who once again peered at Frog's egg.

"You always managed to wake me up with a shock," Frog said, waving his hand in front of Kryl's face again. "But you don't even know I'm here. How do I wake *you* up?"

Frog followed Kryl's gaze to the egg. *His* egg.

"That's it!" he cried. "Kryl, if you give as many hoots about me as you say you do, you're going to find it all sorts of shocking when I do this…"

Frog grabbed the egg. Then he hoisted it high above his head, and sent it crashing to the floor.

As the egg shattered, Kryl screamed. "NoOOoooo—!"

The Decision

Frog sat up and opened his eyes to see Kryl, sitting up and staring back at him.

"Kryl! You're all right!" he cried. "You *are* all right, right?"

"Frog…" she gasped. "You saved me…"

Frog shrugged.

"Pfff — I saved you, I saved the princess — and just now I sort of saved everybody else," he said. "You should see all the saving I've got planned for next week."

Kryl flung her arms around Frog and squeezed him so tightly he thought his head might pop. Princess Rainbow, Nigel and Sheriff Explosion were quick to join in, and soon the entire Defeat All Foes Team were embroiled in one enormous hug. Except Man-Lor, who joined in from a distance, wrapping his own arms around himself.

"Man-Lor is happy," he said. "I am Man-Lor."

With the Defeat All Foes Team complete once more, Frog set about putting things right. He gathered them together with the bragons and the Kroakans.

"I was thinking about the rarewolf's prophecy," he said. "I think maybe I should save the world now."

"I think that would be a wonderful idea," smiled Kryl.

"So, for my first order, I command all Kroakans to pack up their traceships and leave Kingdomland!" Frog declared. "Send them all back to Kroakas. And get me some sandwiches! Anything except turnip…"

"At once, Your Majesty," replied Major Krung, and made her way back into the Farthership.

Frog smiled. "I'm telling you, Kryl, being

King is the easiest business ever!" he said.

"It's a good start, but this is bigger than Kingdomland," Kryl began. "King Kroak sent a thousand armies to a thousand worlds. Those worlds are being conquered as we speak."

"But ... can't I just order them to leave, too?" Frog asked.

"It may not be that simple," Kryl explained. "The sons of King Kroak will not be happy to surrender their worlds. Don't forget, they have all been trained as merciless conquerors, and you are ordering peace. You may have a *rebellion* on your hands..."

"Pfff – I'll bring out their inner champions! You'll see, I'm going to peace-up the whole universe! I'm going to ... going to..." Frog trailed off. He looked around and sighed a long sigh. "I'm going to have to *leave*, aren't I?" he said. "I'm going to have to leave Kingdomland."

The Legend Begins Anew

Wen I grow Up
by Frog
(Aged No Years and a quorter)

Wen I grow Up I don't know wat
I am going to be.
You can't reelly be anything
when the Wurld has Ended.
I can't be a prince or a night
or a traveling sailsman
or a potayto farmur
or a volcano-putter-outer
or a mighty champeun.
So I supose I'll just be me.

"Silly Greeny! You can't leave Kin'domland!" the princess protested. She pointed to the Kroakans as they made their way back up into the Farthership. "The ay'luns can go home on their own. We have to stay together because we're the Pretty Princess Lovely Biscuit Team! In fact, I command you can't go. I command you stay here and ... be my friend."

Frog smiled. "I'll still be your friend, even if I'm a million miles away ... maybe even a hundred," he assured her. "But I'm a full-on outer-space ruler now. I've got heaps of saving stuff to do. And I get the big spaceship, so..."

"But I don't have any other friends," the princess said, kicking the scorched earth with her foot.

"Oh, really?" Frog added. He pointed

behind her. There was Nigel and Susan (who for some reason were holding claws with each other) plus Old 'n' Graham and the remaining bragons, all waving back at them. "I bet they all want to be friends with the *actual* Princess Rainbow."

"They can live at the palace!" she squealed with excitement. "They can be my special proper royal friends! We can do tea parties and dressing up and play with my pocket mummy and daddy!"

Princess Rainbow raced over to the bragons, eager to give them the good news. Frog shook his head and laughed.

Before long, fresh pots of tea had been brewed and Frog, Princess Rainbow, Nigel, Man-Lor, Kryl and the bragons drank to their lost comrades with a cup of tea. Then the princess made a special toast to her "fluffiest, wuffiest, bestest pet ever". Frog smiled and raised his cup to the rarewolf.

"So, are you sure you're ready for this, Frog?" Kryl asked. "Are you sure you're ready to be King ... to take on the universe?"

"Ready? I'm The Mighty Frog! It's my *destiny*," he replied.

Kryl saw something gripped in Frog's hand – a small cube with a green button set into one side.

"What's that?" she asked.

"This? This is..." he began. He peered at the button for a moment, and then slipped it into his pocket. "Just in case."

With that, Frog turned and made his way towards the Farthership.

"Wait a minotaur!" he cried suddenly. "What about—"

"Baa."

Frog spun around to see Sheriff Explosion
trot out of the crowd towards him. He knelt
down and ruffled the sheep's woolly fleece as
it nuzzled his chest.

"I could never forget you, Sheriff! Trusty
steeds don't come along every day," he said.
Then he stood up slowly. "But this is where
we go our separate ways. Sheeps don't belong
in the outer-space place — it's a full-on void
of blackness and cold. I'm setting you free,
Sheriff. Go ... chew grass ... do sheep stuff
... find a Mrs Sheriff and make lots of little
Explosions. You're free!"

"Baa?" bleated Sheriff Explosion. He
stared at Frog for a long moment ... and
then turned to go.

"Pfff — like I could save the universe
without my trusty steed!" Frog cried. He
grabbed the sheep under his arm, drew

his invincible sword and raced up into the Farthership. "Come on, Sheriff Explosion! The legend begins anew!"

"Baa…" sighed the sheep.

THE LEGEND OF FROG

Hear's a bit from the very beginning ...
before all the stuff happuns that just happund ..

The Island on the Edge of the End of the World

Frog replaced his quill pen in the inkpot. "Now for Chapter Two."

"What are you writing, Frog?"

Frog slammed his book shut. He turned to see Buttercup's head poking round the door. She looked nothing like Frog. She did not share his bright, mottled green skin or his bulbous yellow eyes. She had ears and a nose – which Frog lacked – and long, brown hair, while Frog had not a single hair on his head. In fact, Buttercup looked decidedly human – there wasn't a hint of anything amphibian about her. But then Buttercup had not hatched from a golden egg.

"I'm – uh – I'm just writing down our

story," replied Frog. "About the golden egg and the mighty prince."

"It's most royal of you to practise your quill-craft," she said, "but it's past both our bedtimes and we have a big day tomorrow: the flower needs watering, the potato needs picking, the clouds need counting…"

"We did all that yesterday – and the day before," huffed Frog.

"We could always practise your camouflage," Buttercup suggested.

"What do I have to hide from? There's no one here but us," said Frog, unleashing a loud and deliberate sigh. He hopped down from his chair and into bed.

"So, what story would you like?" said Buttercup, as she tucked him in. "I could tell you about the time I rode the Queen's newnicorns? Or the time the King out-farted the imp-O-lights? Or when the sunbirds gave the Queen a ray of light for her birthday?" She glanced at Frog's story. "Or about the golden egg that hatched a mighty prince…"

"You could tell me about the End of the World," Frog said.

"Again? There's nothing more to tell," Buttercup sighed, rubbing her eyes. "Scorched earth … blackened skies … catastrophe."

"Catastrophe," repeated Frog, in a reverie. "Does anyone live there?"

"Of course not," sighed Buttercup. "How could anyone live at the End of the World?"

"I don't know, it's just — I'm a prince," said Frog. "Do I really have to stay on this island forever? It feels like I'm meant for something more … princely."

Buttercup stiffened. She took a deep

breath and looked at her feet. By the time she looked up she had put on a smile. "What did you dream last night? Do you remember?" she asked.

Frog remembered his not uncommon dream immediately. "I was in the sky, higher than everything, higher than the stars, looking down on the world," he replied.

"Did it feel real?" she asked. Frog nodded. "So, can you fly higher than the stars?"

"No, but—"

"No. Just because you feel something doesn't make it real," said Buttercup quickly. "You were destined to be a great ruler, Frog — I'm sure you would have been. But that world is gone. The World has Ended. We and this island are all that is left. I brought you here and built you a home and kept you safe. It's just you and me, forever and ever."

"I know, but … forever is ages," huffed Frog.

Buttercup let out a chuckle. "You're a good boy, Frog," she said, kissing him on the head.

Frog knew what she would say as she put out the lamp – she had said the same thing every night since he'd hatched from his golden egg.

"Sleep well, Royal Majesty, Lord of all Kingdoms, Rightful Ruler of the World … Prince Frog."

Have you read...

Guy Bass

Stitch Head

In CASTLE GROTTESKEW

something BIG
is about to happen...

...to someone SMALL.

Join a mad professor's forgotten
creation as he steps out of the
shadows into the adventure
of an almost-lifetime...

Guy Bass

STITCH HEAD

The Pirate's Eye

Someone
SMALL
is about
to set sail
on a
BIG
adventure.

Join a mad professor's forgotten
creation as he prepares for an
almost-life on the high seas.

Guy Bass

Stitch Head

The Ghost of Grotteskew

Someone
SMALL
is about to
discover a
BIG
secret.

Join a mad professor's
forgotten creation as he fights
for his heart and soul…

Guy Bass

STITCH HEAD

THE SPIDER'S LAIR

Someone
SMALL
is about to
get into
BIG
trouble.

Join a mad professor's
forgotten creation as he gets
caught up in a web of mystery…

Guy Bass is an award-winning author whose children's books include *Secret Agent: Agent of X.M.A.S*, the *Dinkin Dings* series and, most recently, the highly acclaimed *Stitch Head* series. In 2010, *Dinkin Dings and the Frightening Things* won the CBBC Blue Peter Award in the 'Most Fun Story with Pictures' category. Guy's books have also won a number of local book awards.

Guy has also written plays for both adults and children. He has previously been a theatre producer, illustrator and has acted his way out of several paper bags.

Guy lives in London with his wife. He enjoys long walks on toast and the smell of a forgetful sparrow.